Alaska
State Facts

Nicknames:	Last Frontier, Great Land, Land of the Midnight Sun
Date Entered Union:	January 3, 1959 (the 49th state)
Motto:	North to the future
Alaska Men:	William A. Egan, *first state governor* Charles E. Bunnell, *educator* Joseph Juneau, *prospector* John Griffith (Jack) London, *author*
Flower:	Forget-me-not
Tree:	Sitka spruce
Bird:	Willow ptarmigan
Song:	"Alaska's Flag"
State Name's Origin:	Based on Eskimo word *alakshak*, meaning "great lands" or "peninsula."
Fun Fact:	The state of Rhode Island could fit into Alaska 425 times.

and mommy

WIFE ^ WANTED

NO ROMANCE NECESSARY

APPLY BOX 6757
NOWHERE, ALASKA

The Bride Came C.O.D.

BARBARA BRETTON

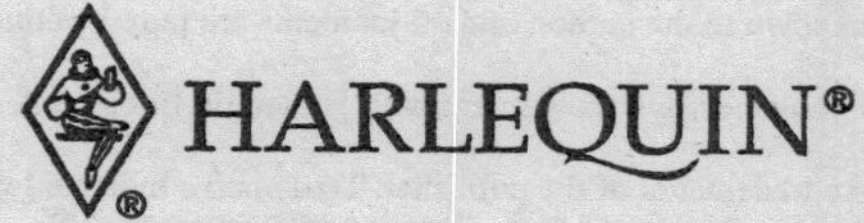

TORONTO • NEW YORK • LONDON
AMSTERDAM • PARIS • SYDNEY • HAMBURG
STOCKHOLM • ATHENS • TOKYO • MILAN • MADRID
PRAGUE • WARSAW • BUDAPEST • AUCKLAND

For Barbara "The Fax-Meister" Schenck,
who knows a good roadhouse when she sees one

HARLEQUIN BOOKS
225 Duncan Mill Road, Don Mills,
Ontario, Canada M3B 3K9

ISBN 0-373-82200-6

THE BRIDE CAME C.O.D.

This edition published by arrangement with Harlequin Books S.A.

Visit us at www.eHarlequin.com

Printed in U.S.A.

About the Author

With over eight million copies of her books in print worldwide, **Barbara Bretton** enjoys a warm place in the hearts of romance readers everywhere. After thirty-plus contemporary and historical novels, this bestselling author is listed in *Foremost Women in the Twentieth Century,* and has been honored with numerous writing awards, including *Romantic Times Magazine* Reviewer's Choice Awards and a Silver Pen Award from *Affaire de Coeur.* Barbara is a two-time nominee for the *Romantic Times Magazine* Storyteller of the Year.

Books by Barbara Bretton

Harlequin American Romance

Love Changes #3
The Sweetest of Debts #49
No Safe Place #91
The Edge of Forever #138
Promises in the Night #161
Shooting Star #175
**Playing for Time* #193
Second Harmony #211
Nobody's Baby #230
**Honeymoon Hotel* #251
**A Fine Madness* #274
Mother Knows Best #305
Mrs. Scrooge #322
**All We Know of Heaven* #355
Sentimental Journey #365
Stranger in Paradise #369
Bundle of Joy #393
Daddy's Girl #441
Renegade Lover #493
**The Bride Came C.O.D.* #505
The Invisible Groom #554
Operation: Husband #581
Operation: Baby #689

* PAX series

MIRA

Tomorrow & Always
No Safe Place
Destiny's Child
Shooting Star
Starfire
Guilty Pleasures

Dear Reader,

Don't tell anybody, but sometimes writing is so much fun that I'm ashamed to call it work. Every now and then a book comes along that is filled with such lovable characters that I can't wait to get up in the morning and see what they've been up to while I slept.

When I created the PAX series for Harlequin American Romance (more years ago than I care to admit), I knew I was onto something special. Through PAX, a supersecret spy organization I fondly call The Gang That Couldn't Shoot Straight, I've been able to write adventures, comedies and four-hanky tearjerkers, with a cast of characters who feel more like good friends than imaginary heroes and heroines.

The Bride Came C.O.D. is the fifth in the series, a comedy set in Nowhere, Alaska—a tiny town in the middle of (you guessed it) nowhere. Not at all the kind of place where you'd expect to find socialite Lexi Marsden arriving as a mail-order bride. Kiel Brown is a single father and a brilliant scientist who is having more trouble than he can shake a nuclear reactor at just keeping up with the laundry. Just how does a man manage to balance saving the world with peanut-butter-and-jelly dinners for daddy and daughter?

He doesn't, that's how. Kiel needs a wife same as Kelsey needs a mother and Lexi is exactly what they've been looking for.

Or is she?

I'm afraid you're going to have to sit down, put your feet up and read *The Bride Came C.O.D.* to find out! You can find me at: Barbara Bretton, 601 Route 206—Suite #26442, Belle Mead NJ 08502. I'd love to hear from you.

With affection,

Barbara

Prologue

Nowhere, Alaska

"Tell me I didn't hear that," said the male voice on the other end of the telephone. "Tell me I'm wrong."

"She's here," Kiel Brown repeated for the third time, "and she's staying here."

"She can't stay," said the frazzled PAX coordinator. "She's not part of the plan."

"She's part of my plan," said Kiel through gritted teeth.

"I thought she was staying with your cousin in Chicago."

"My aunt in Boston. She's not staying there any longer."

"Ship her back."

"Can't do," said Kiel. "My aunt broke her leg."

"So?" said the PAX coordinator. The man was a Ph.D. in foreign affairs, a Rhodes scholar—and an unqualified moron.

"You don't know much about four-year-old girls, do you?" Kiel retorted. "My aunt would commit hara-kiri." As it was, his aunt Edith had sounded relieved to send Kelsey back home. ''I'm too old for this,'' she had told Kiel from her hospital bed. ''Little girls were less...active in my day.''

''There must be someone else,'' the coordinator said in a maddeningly logical tone of voice.

''There isn't.''

''Cousins...brothers...sisters... Help me with this, Brown.''

Kiel finally exploded. ''You're a spy organization, damn it. You know there's no one else to take care of Kelsey.''

''Ship her down here to Connecticut and we'll find someone to watch out for her until you've completed your assignment.''

''The hell I will. This is my daughter you're talking about, not a package for FedEx. She's here and she's staying here and if you have trouble with that, we can call the whole thing off right now.''

He slammed the phone down so hard that the plastic cradle snapped in two, sending shards skittering across the polished wood floor of the kitchen. It felt good but not half as good as heaving the damn thing out the window would feel.

PAX needed him more than he needed them. He was the top man in his field. No one else was even close.

If PAX wanted him to provide the solution, they'd have to take the entire package, Kelsey included.

Grimly he counted down the minutes until they called back. Four. Three. Two.

''I hope you guys aren't always this predictable,''

he said when he picked up the ringing phone, "or democracy is in big trouble."

"Can the sarcasm," said a familiar voice. Ryder O'Neal, current head of the entire operation, was known for his hardheaded pragmatism and his surprisingly soft heart. He had taken over for Alistair Chambers when Chambers retired to a farm in Scotland with his beautiful actress/wife Holland. "Joanna and I have two kids of our own. I know what you're up against."

"I'm not sending my daughter away."

"Nobody's going to ask you to. We're here to make it easy for you to do your job."

"If you meant that, you wouldn't have sent me off to the back of beyond."

"You know as well as I do that security is our primary objective." O'Neal paused. "Your security as well as the security of the project. The best thing for everyone concerned is to have you in relative seclusion."

Nowhere, Alaska, had qualified on most counts, at least until Kelsey arrived. In a few short weeks his daughter had attracted more attention than the arrival of a UFO complete with alien crew. People who had viewed his arrival on the scene with little more than polite curiosity now flocked to him with covered-dish casseroles and phone numbers of single women who would love to change their status.

Mrs. Loomis at the general store tsk-tsked each time he came in for supplies. "A man like you doin' the chores and carin' for a little one. Woman's work, that's what it is.'' She batted her faded blue eyes at him as if volunteering for the job.

Old Mr. Packer who ran the filling station dispensed gas and bad advice each time he topped up the tank of Kiel's Jeep Cherokee. ''You need a wife up here, boy. You ain't been here for one of our winters. Need someone to keep you warm at night.''

Even Imelda Mulroney, who'd moved back into town not long after Kiel's arrival, said Kiel couldn't go on the way he was going much longer. ''Winter's comin','' Imelda said in the ominous tones everyone used when talking about the changing of the seasons. ''My hubby and me got a cabin out in the bush just like yours and I'm here to tell you it ain't easy out there, especially with a little one.''

Imelda had a point. They all did, even if Kiel didn't want to admit it. Kelsey was all energy and curiosity, a quicksilver blend of everything that had been wonderful between him and her mother, if only for a little while.

Kelsey hadn't been back with him a week before he discovered that an IQ of one hundred and seventy-five and a Ph.D. in nuclear physics were no help when it came to caring for a child in the middle of the wilderness. He struggled with ''Sesame Street'' by day and nuclear fusion by night and slept one hour out of every twenty-four.

''You guys are tying my hands,'' Kiel said with as much control as he could manage. ''The nearest day-care center is one hundred and twenty miles away. If you'd let me hire a housekeeper to watch Kelsey, I could get back to work.''

O'Neal's response was both earthy and to the point. "We can't risk it. We have reason to believe there are operatives in your vicinity. I don't have to explain the ramifications if your research should fall into the wrong hands."

"Everyone in this damn town keeps telling me I need a wife. If that would keep them from dropping by, I'd put an ad on one of those computer bulletin boards. 'Lonely Nuclear Scientist Needs Spouse. No Romance Necessary.'"

"Maybe you should."

"Right," said Kiel. "You won't let me hire a housekeeper but you'd let me marry a stranger."

"As long as we provided the stranger."

"Since when is PAX in the matchmaking business?"

"Since about three minutes ago. We need you and we'll do whatever it takes to keep you happy."

"Including finding me a wife?"

"Including finding you a wife."

"You're a great bunch of guys," said Kiel, unable to mask the edge in his voice, "but I don't want a wife." He'd been married once and badly. He wasn't about to do it again.

"Like you said, Kiel, we're not talking romance here. We're talking convenience."

"A housekeeper is convenient."

"A housekeeper won't keep the ladies of Nowhere from trying to find you a wife."

"How do I keep *you* from finding me a wife?"

Ryder laughed.

Kiel didn't.

"It'll work out," Ryder said an hour later after the details had been worked out.

"Right," said Kiel as a black cloud of doom settled over him. "Isn't that what they said to Custer?"

Chapter One

En route to Nowhere

Marrying a man she didn't know wasn't the craziest thing Lexi Marsden had ever heard of.

Jumping out of airplanes was crazy. Swimming with sharks was crazy. Running with bulls, eating goldfish, and walking through Central Park at midnight were all crazy.

People did crazy things every day of the week and lived to tell the tale. Why should she be any different? She was just getting married, after all, not joining the army. The army tied you up for three years. If everything went according to her plan, this marriage would be over in six months.

She stared out the window of the tiny seaplane as it skimmed across the endless miles of wilderness called Alaska. The only available male willing to contemplate marriage without romance and he had to live in a place called Nowhere. Wouldn't you just know it?

When Joanna Stratton O'Neal called yesterday afternoon to broach the topic, Lexi had bombarded her friend with questions.

"I never did understand exactly what you and Ryder do for a living," she had said. She'd always believed it to be some kind of government contract work. "You're environmentalists?"

"Among other things."

"Sounds more like you're matchmakers."

"When necessary."

She'd listened as Joanna swore to her that despite its name, Nowhere was really a respectable small town in Alaska.

"No Bloomingdale's," Joanna had said with a laugh, "but I can guarantee indoor plumbing, a microwave oven and a satellite dish."

"No Bloomingdale's," Lexi repeated, only half kidding. "I don't know..."

You have no choice, that irritating little voice inside her head had whined. *If you want what belongs to you, you have to go through with it.*

Time was running out. In three weeks it would be too late. She would turn twenty-five and her inheritance would be locked in trust until her fortieth birthday.

What choice did she have? She had to get married and she had to do it now, even if it meant leaving behind civilization as she knew it.

"His name is Kiel Brown," Joanna had continued, "and he's in environmental research."

Lexi groaned. "Does that mean I can't bring my sable?"

"I'll pretend you didn't say that."

"What is he like?"

"Sky-high IQ, bookish." Joanna had paused a moment. "And he's not looking for a wife in the... traditional sense." She went on to explain that Mr. Kiel Brown was getting tired of being bombarded with proposals, indecent and otherwise, from the ladies of Nowhere and an arranged marriage seemed like the best solution.

Lexi had been ecstatic.

No sex. No romance. It was enough to make a woman believe in destiny.

"There is one drawback," Joanna had said carefully. "Kiel has a daughter."

I can handle that, Lexi told herself over and over again. How hard can it be? The absentminded professor could lock himself away in his laboratory and log migratory patterns of Alaskan birds while Lexi and his little girl amused themselves with hair ribbons and fairy tales.

Six months was all she needed. Six months and one day to collect her inheritance. They'd get married, they'd have it annulled, she'd become an heiress. It couldn't be more perfect.

She leaned forward and tapped the pilot on the shoulder. "I have a question."

"Fire away," said the pilot, a brawny character named MacDougal. She'd been expecting a pilot named Jensen but apparently he'd broken his leg the night before. "If I don't know the answer, I'll find someone who does."

"Do you have any children?"

"Six," said MacDougal with a laugh. "Two in college, two in grad school, two out of the house."

"I don't suppose you remember much of what they were like when they were little."

"Long time ago," he said, twisting around in his seat to look at her. "How come?"

"Just curious," she said. He continued to look at her and she motioned toward the instrument panel. "Shouldn't you keep your eyes on the road, so to speak?"

"I've got three grandbabies," he offered, taking a cursory look out the window. "That help any?"

"Only if one of them is a four-year-old girl."

"Bingo!" said MacDougal, turning back to the instrument panel. "My oldest turns four next week."

"How marvelous!" Lexi's mood brightened. "Do you have a photo?"

"Do cats have kittens?" He reached into the front pocket of his flannel shirt and withdrew a thick packet of snapshots. "Annie, Sarah and Lindsay. You could search the lower 48 for the rest of your life and not find cuter kids."

Lexi, who was not a connoisseur of children cute or otherwise, quickly flipped through the stack of photos. Little girls in frilly pastel dresses. Little girls with hair ribbons and shiny patent shoes. Obviously the world hadn't changed that much in the twenty years since she was Kelsey's age. Little girls still loved carriages and baby dolls, all the things Lexi herself had adored as a child.

A bookish intellectual who wanted a wife without

emotional involvement and a little girl who was just like Lexi had been at her age, angelic and obedient.

Life didn't get much better than that.

"No!"

Kiel gritted his teeth and tightened his grip on the hairbrush. "C'mon, Kelse. Don't you want your hair to look nice?"

Kelsey's dark eyes flashed a warning. "NO!"

"So it's going to be one of those days." It figured she'd pick today of all days to throw a tantrum. He placed the hairbrush down atop the dresser. "How about you let me put your hair in a ponytail?"

"I don't like ponytails." She reached for her Red Sox baseball cap and plopped it on her head. "I like this."

She wasn't going to win any fashion awards but that was the least of his worries. Alexa Grace Marsden was due to arrive on their doorstep sometime today and Kiel had hoped Kelsey would at least let him brush her hair for the occasion.

"Pancakes or French toast?" he asked as he scooped her up into his arms.

Her little mouth curved in a grin that was so much like her mother's that his breath caught for an instant. "'cakes."

"Pan-cakes," he said. Helena's diction had been so beautifully precise that he used to say he could listen to her recite the phone book.

"Paaann-caakes."

"You're a wise guy, Kelse," he said as they started

down the hallway toward the kitchen. "Do you know that?"

"No," she said, hugging him around the neck. "I'm a wise girl."

"I'm not going to argue that."

Fatherhood continued to amaze him. He'd always liked kids the same way he liked puppies and kittens and other small things. Smile absently, pat them on the head, then forget they existed. All that had changed the day he'd walked into Helena's office and heard the words, "We're going to have a baby." The reality of fatherhood had barreled over him like a runaway train, obliterating everything in its path. From the first moment when he heard Kelsey's heart beating inside her mother's womb, he'd known instinctively that he would risk his life to keep the two of them safe from harm.

Too bad Helena hadn't felt the same way. When she died in a boating accident off Martha's Vineyard, Kiel had been the second person notified. The man she'd left him for had been the first.

He pushed away the memories and headed for the kitchen, which was located at the back of the cabin. It boasted three windows and a view of Denali in the distance that was second to none. His research lab, a sturdy concrete structure, was a ten-second walk from the back door. It would be the perfect situation for a work-at-home father if the father was a writer or an artist, someone who only had to worry about peanut-butter-and-jelly stains from inquisitive fingers.

When the father-in-question worked with nuclear energy, it was another story.

He sat Kelsey down at the table, then disappeared into the pantry to grab some pancakes out of the freezer.

"No more of these once Lexi gets here," he announced, popping the pancakes into the microwave. "We'll be eating meals the same day they're cooked." He punched a few buttons, then sat down opposite his daughter. "What do you think about that?"

"Cool," said Kelsey, drinking her orange juice from her favorite *Beauty and the Beast* glass.

"Cool?" He started to laugh. "Since when do you say cool?"

"I saw it on TV."

Which was another reason why he had to stop using television as a baby-sitter.

It occurred to him that maybe PAX was right about some things. Kelsey deserved more than temporary housekeepers to mother her. He didn't want a wife, not in the real sense, but he needed a partner. A woman who wasn't looking for hearts and flowers and all the things he no longer had to give. Someone who understood kids and knew when and how to keep her mouth shut when it came to his work.

If the good folks at PAX could provide that, they were miracle workers.

"YOU'RE LANDING HERE?" Lexi's voice rose an octave. "You can't land here! This isn't an airport."

"Sure it is," said MacDougal as the tiny plane nosed downward.

She looked out the window. "All I see is snow."

"Over there." He inclined his head left. "See that stripe in the snow?"

Lexi nodded. "I thought that was a shadow."

MacDougal's laugh rumbled through the cabin. "Some shadow. That's an airstrip and we're about to land on it."

It was amazing how many prayers a woman could remember when her life was about to end. Lexi closed her eyes tightly, crossed herself, then prepared to die.

This is what you get for being greedy, Alexa Grace Marsden. This is your punishment for not marrying Franklin Wade Bainbridge when you had a chance.

Her father had been Franklin's number-one supporter and it wasn't difficult to see why. Franklin was kind, considerate, moderately handsome, wealthy as Croesus. He was perfect husband material for some lucky girl. Preferably one who loved him. Which Lexi didn't. She liked him. She respected him. But she didn't love him and that had made all the difference. She wanted someone wonderful: tall, dark and handsome would be nice. Someone who made her heart beat faster when he came into a room. Someone who wouldn't give in to her every demand...at least, not at first. Someone who would love her to distraction.

Love can grow, her father used to say, *if you give it a chance.* The notion of love at first sight and thunderbolts was the product of an overworked romantic imagination, something Lexi could outgrow.

On the morning of her father's death, he and Lexi had had a long discussion on her unmarried status and he'd lectured her sternly on the fact that Franklin wouldn't wait for her forever.

"Good," Lexi had said sharply. "I hope he finds himself a wonderful woman and lives happily ever after."

She clutched the sides of her seat as the plane bumped its way across the pathetic excuse for a landing strip. *It's not like I didn't ask Franklin,* she thought, trying to ignore the screech of brakes and the way the plane seemed to skid to the right. She'd gone straight from the lawyer's office to Franklin's club after the reading of her father's will and laid the whole story out for him. "I made a mistake," she'd said as he stared at her in disbelief. "You can marry me after all. I'll make it well worth your while."

The memory of the horrified look on his face still managed to make her blush. The story quickly spread throughout their set and before sundown she had three proposals from male acquaintances, none of whom were willing to have a marriage in name only.

Finally it had occurred to her that she was looking in all the wrong places for Mr. Right. The last thing she wanted was a strong man with a healthy libido. What she needed was a nerd. A pleasant nerd. One who would rather spend his time tinkering at a computer keyboard than practicing the Kama Sutra.

Exactly like the nerd Joanna had offered to her last night.

Oh, Joanna hadn't called him a nerd but she didn't have to say the word for Lexi to get the picture in three-dimensional detail. The man counted birds and moose for a living. Didn't that about say it all?

She tapped MacDougal on the shoulder again. "Are there many spotted musk deer around here?"

"Beats me," said MacDougal, unhitching his seat belt and standing up. "I'm not much for wildlife myself unless it's marinated and on the grill." He rose to his feet and stretched. "Why'd you ask?"

"The man I'm marrying is doing a long-term study of their migratory patterns."

MacDougal snorted as he flung open the door and a gust of cold air made her shiver. "A pretty girl like you marrying one of those tree huggers? Seems like a waste to me."

"Thank you," she said, gathering her belongings, "but he's exactly what I'm looking for."

"No accountin' for taste." MacDougal leaped to the ground and helped her from the plane. "Now let's talk about the bill."

FIRST THERE WAS the uproar over the plane fare, then MacDougal decided to send her driver packing and take her to her final destination herself. Which probably shouldn't have surprised Lexi because the man was already two hundred dollars in the red and growing more agitated about it by the second.

"If you took American Express, we wouldn't have this problem," she pointed out as she climbed into the Jeep.

"I take Visa," he said, "but you don't have it."

"Visa is...common," she said, buckling her seat belt.

"What about MasterCard?"

"That too."

"So we have a problem," said MacDougal, sliding behind the wheel.

"My fiancé will straighten things out," she said loftily. "You'll see."

"I'd better see," said MacDougal.

"You were much nicer before this problem with money came up."

"Back then I could afford to be."

They were silent for a few agonizing minutes. It seemed like a thousand years to Lexi. Finally she couldn't take the silence any longer and she began to prattle on about her upcoming marriage, sounding for all the world like a blushing bride with the wedding night on her mind.

"What's that?" she asked, pointing toward a clump of buildings to her left.

"Nowhere," said MacDougal. "Blink twice and you'll think you imagined it."

"That's the town?"

"None other."

"You don't even have a traffic light."

He glanced at her through the rearview mirror. "Ain't needed one so far."

Lexi was beside herself by the time the driver guided the Jeep up the rutted road that led to her new home.

"I'm afraid to look," she said, hands over her eyes. "How bad is it?"

MacDougal brought the Jeep to a halt. "You could do worse."

Considering what she'd seen of Nowhere so far, that was hardly comforting. Cautiously she peered between her fingers.

A stand of pine trees towered majestically to her

left. Another stand of pine trees towered equally majestically to her right. In the middle of those pine trees was a one-story log cabin that looked as though it belonged on a postcard of New England. A beat-up old car and a new Jeep were parked in what passed for a driveway.

"Well," she said, taking note of the huge windows in the front and the well-tended walkway, "I suppose I could have done worse."

Again a curious look from the driver.

"Is there something wrong?" she snapped, unnerved by his scrutiny. "You keep looking at me like I have two heads."

"You talk enough for two heads," said MacDougal. "I don't think I ever saw a woman got so much to say about nothin'."

She glowered at him. "Has anyone ever told you it's rude to insult a paying customer?"

"Lady, so far you're not a payin' customer. You owe me four hundred and fifty dollars." He didn't bat an eye. "Plus tip."

"That's highway robbery!"

"Hell, no," he said. "We just spent two hours on the road and it'll take me another two to get back, at sixty-five dollars per. Then there's the plane fare. I'm cuttin' you a deal."

"I already told you I don't have that much cash. You'll have to speak with my fiancé." *Joanna,* she thought, *I could strangle you.* Why hadn't her friend made it clear her organization wasn't footing the bills?

The walkway had been shoveled but patches of ice

still clung to the stones. Obviously high heels were not the normal footwear around here. She knocked on the door, waited five seconds, then knocked again.

"Oh, come on," she muttered, aware of MacDougal's intense scrutiny. She banged harder on the door. He was probably up to his eyeballs in research books, fumbling with his bifocals, smoothing his baggy cords, stepping over his daughter's baby dolls.

She heard the sound of footsteps.

She straightened her shoulders.

The door swung open and the biggest, most beautiful man she'd ever seen in her life appeared before her eyes. She prayed it wasn't her husband-to-be.

SHE'S NOT THE ONE, he silently pleaded with fate. *She can't be.*

She was altogether too little and too useless-looking for Kiel's taste, like a hood ornament on a fancy sports car instead of a real-live woman. She wore high heels, a white wool coat that would never survive an hour with Kelsey and a headful of sleek blond hair that probably took all day to arrange. The kind of woman who'd use up a month's worth of hot water with one lazy bubble bath.

"Are you going to say something," he snapped, feeling entirely unlike his usual self, "or are you going to bang on the door again?"

"I'm Alexa Grace Marsden and I need four hundred and fifty dollars," she blurted out with a defiant lift of her chin. Her china-blue eyes flashed with fire.

"Yeah?" The statement was so absurd he laughed in her face. "Don't look at me."

"I'd prefer not to," she said with the arrogance of the born aristocrat. "If you'd direct me to Kiel Brown, you can go about your business."

Geez, O'Neal, he thought. *What the hell have you gotten me into?*

He glanced at his cabin. Nothing short of Buckingham Palace would be big enough for the two of them. She'd tear through a truckload of generators just running her hair dryer. Either PAX was coming up with better covers for their operatives or this chick was the most unlikely spy since Boris and Natasha.

"Stop looking at me like that!" She stamped her foot on the hard-packed snow. The last time he'd seen a grown woman stamp her foot was in one of those screwball comedies from the thirties with the spoiled-brat heroines and dashing heroes who invariably fell in love with them.

Not much chance of that.

She was still yapping. "—and if you think I'm going to put up with such insolence from the hired help when I'm living here, you're mad. You can consider yourself—"

He started to laugh. "Fired?"

She looked as if she wanted to hit him with her Gucci purse. "Yes," she said, her high cheekbones stained with color. "Fired."

"I don't think so."

Her eyes narrowed. "You think well of yourself for a handyman."

"I'm not a handyman," he said, pulling her into his embrace. "I'm the man you're here to marry."

And then he did what he had to do.

He kissed her.

Chapter Two

He pulled her into his arms as if he owned her.

Lexi opened her mouth to scream but his mouth slanted across hers and the scream lodged in her throat.

His mouth was hard. His lips were soft. He smelled of soap and spice and something infinitely more appealing. Crushed up against his body, she felt overwhelmed by a force greater than herself.

There was something terrifying about being held by a man the size of a redwood tree…and something exciting.

Oh yes.

Exciting.

He had no business kissing her. Or holding her that tightly. If she could just gather her wits about her, she'd kick him in the shins or slap his face or knee him in the groin. She wasn't stupid or powerless.

But she didn't move.

And he didn't stop kissing her.

"Put your arms around me," he murmured against her lips. "He's watching."

She glanced over his shoulder at MacDougal who was making his way up the path toward them.

"Now!" How he could murmur in such a threatening tone of voice was beyond her. Cautiously she placed her hands against his chest. Dear God, he was solid as a wall of granite and about as malleable.

"Act like we're in love or the whole damn town will know the truth before the sun goes down."

Her sanity returned. "Don't you dare tell me what to do! I'll—"

"How about savin' that for later," MacDougal interrupted. "I've gotta get back to the airfield before sunset and at the rate you're goin', I don't stand much of a chance." He looked from Lexi to Kiel, then back again. "So is your hubby gonna pay your bill or is he sendin' you back where you came from?"

"Don't tempt me," she heard Kiel mutter under his breath. The fact that she didn't kick him was a testament to the education she'd received at finishing school.

She favored MacDougal with her best smile. "Of course my fiancé will pay my bill." She linked her arm through Kiel's. For an environmentalist he had a very unscholarly arrangement of muscles underneath his plaid shirt. "Kiel knows I just have no mind when it comes to money." *Only because I don't have any…at least not yet.* When she came into her inheritance, she intended to be a veritable financial wizard.

"Lady," said MacDougal, "I don't much care if you can't add two and two. I just want my money."

"You didn't bring any money?" asked Kiel.

She considered dimpling but thought better of it.

She had a feeling her future husband didn't put much store in feminine wiles. She opted for a sincere smile. "If you'd be so kind as to pay Mr. MacDougal, you can bring my luggage inside."

"You *are* kidding, aren't you?"

The smile faltered but she inched it up another notch. "Do I look as if I'm kidding?"

His eyebrows knotted. The man obviously knew how to glower with the best of them. "You don't have any money?"

She sighed loudly. Six months was beginning to sound like a life sentence. "Not enough obviously. Now if you'd just take care of it, we can continue this argument in private."

IT OCCURRED to Kiel that he could kill her right there on the spot and there wasn't a jury in the country that would convict him. MacDougal was looking at him as if he'd rather walk all the way back to the airport than be in Kiel's shoes.

"I don't have that kind of cash on me," he said to the driver. "Will you take a check?"

MacDougal nodded.

"Come on in," Kiel said. "My checkbook's inside."

MacDougal waited in the front room while Kiel got the checkbook from the bedroom.

"You really goin' to marry her?" MacDougal asked as Kiel wrote out a check.

Kiel grunted.

"She'll run you a merry race, that one," said MacDougal. "Talked five hours straight without takin' a breath.'' He pocketed the check. ''She's mighty cute to look at but I wouldn't marry her on a bet.''

Yeah, thought Kiel. *At least you have a choice.*

MacDougal had left Lexi's bags at the edge of the road. Lexi was still standing next to them.

Kiel approached her. ''Grab what you can and I'll take the rest.''

She looked at him as if he were speaking in tongues. ''Can't you make two trips?''

He started down the walkway. ''No,'' he said over his shoulder. ''I can't.''

THE FUNNY THING WAS, he really meant it.

Lexi watched in growing amazement as he picked up her three matching leather Pullman cases and carried them into the house as if they were packed with feathers. Her makeup case, overnight bag and accessories box were still resting on a pile of snow near the road.

Surely he'd come back for them. He couldn't possibly expect her to walk down there in her high heels and drag everything inside.

She wrapped her cashmere coat more closely around her body and waited. What on earth was taking him so long? All he had to do was deposit the suitcases in her room and come back outside. For all he knew, she could have slipped on a treacherous patch of ice and have been lying there bleeding and in pain.

She tapped her foot impatiently as the seconds turned into minutes. A fierce wind whipped her hair across her eyes and she brushed it away with a sharp gesture. The fifteenth of September, and already there was a layer of snow on the ground. What on earth would it be like come December?

The thought didn't bear closer inspection.

KIEL PEERED OUT at her from the living-room window.

"What the hell are you going to do," he muttered, "stand there all day?"

She wasn't exactly dressed for it. Spiky high heels and snow weren't a great combination. And that fancy white coat of hers looked as though it would come apart at the first stiff breeze. In his experience PAX operatives could be many things, pigheaded and annoying among them, but they were never unprepared.

He'd expected a competent, no-nonsense type of woman, one who at least came equipped with a polypropylene shirt, Gore-tex mountaineering mittens and blizzard-proof boots.

"Daddy?"

He looked down to see Kelsey tugging at his sleeve. She'd tugged her baseball cap on over her tousled hair and her long-sleeved T-shirt had obviously seen better days.

"There's a princess outside."

He scooped her up in his arms. "Where?" he asked. As if he didn't know.

Sure enough. Kelsey pointed toward Little Miss Obnoxious who was still cooling her heels outside. "She has blond hair," Kelsey said. "All princesses have blond hair."

He looked at his dark-haired daughter. "The most beautiful princesses have hair just like yours," he said, planting a kiss on top of her baseball cap. God save him from spy-princesses with attitude problems.

Kelsey, however, was having none of that. "Everyone knows princesses have hair like Princess Diana." She met his eyes and he swore he could see every single digit of her considerable IQ zeroing in on him. "She kissed you."

Not exactly the way it happened but close enough. "You saw that?"

Kelsey nodded vigorously. "Why did she kiss you?"

"Remember I told you that someone was coming to live with us to take care of you while I'm working?"

She nodded again. "A mommy, but not really."

His throat tightened with emotion. "That's right. She'll be with us as long as we live in Alaska."

"But why did she kiss you?"

"That's a long story, Kelse." And one he wasn't about to tackle.

"I want to know."

He took a deep breath. "She was saying hello."

"When Mr. Packer says hello, he doesn't kiss you."

"And I'm grateful."

Kelsey looked out the window again. "Isn't she cold?"

"I don't know." She was probably too stubborn to admit it.

"Can we let her in?"

"I suppose we have to, don't we?"

Kelsey nodded. "It's almost lunchtime."

"Get your coat," he said, putting her down, "and we'll bring the rest of her things inside."

HE WAS WATCHING HER.

Lexi didn't have to turn around to know that the rat was watching her from the warmth of his ridiculous log cabin. And she didn't need a Ph.D. from Harvard to know that he wasn't going to come back outside and help her with her luggage.

"Kiel can be a bit...difficult," Joanna had said when she saw Lexi off at JFK less than twenty-four hours ago. "Geniuses are not your normal breed of cat."

You don't know the half of it, Lexi thought, shivering beneath her flimsy coat. He was rude, inconsiderate and too darn handsome for his own good and she intended to tell him exactly that.

If she ever saw him again.

Of course, she might not mention the "too darn handsome" part. He seemed to be conceited enough as it was. Wouldn't you think Joanna could have had the decency to let her know that the environmental genius could give Selleck and Costner a run for their money?

Not that it mattered. She wasn't here for romance, even if his unexpected kiss had taken her by surprise. At least at first. There was something undeniably romantic about being swept into the arms of a brawny stranger, but his rotten disposition had quickly put an end to any fantasies she might have been foolish enough to entertain.

She was here to be a wife-in-name-only for the next six months and the minute she fulfilled the requirements of her father's last will and testament, she'd be on the next plane from Nowhere and headed back to civilization.

A strong wind knocked her back on her heels and her resolve wavered. Succumbing to frostbite hadn't been part of her master plan. Okay, let him be a heartless, thoughtless monster. That was his problem. Lexi was going to take the high road and march right into that house and try again.

She turned abruptly and nearly fell over a very tiny person clad in a bright red parka and a navy blue baseball cap.

"I'm Kelsey," the child said. "Are you a princess?"

Chalk up another surprise, Joanna, she thought wryly. *His daughter is a little boy.*

"No, I'm not a princess," she said, bending down to inspect the snag on her ivory hose.

"Then who are you?"

"Alexa Grace Marsden." She extended her hand, realized how absurd it was, but pressed onward. "Would you like to shake my hand?"

Kelsey nodded. The tiny hand was engulfed by Lexi's and she felt an odd fluttering in the pit of her stomach at the thought that she would be responsible for this child—if only temporarily.

"Aren't you cold?" Kelsey asked.

"Yes," said Lexi. "I'm freezing."

"Why are you standing outside?"

Because your daddy is a heartless monster, that's why. She pointed toward the luggage stacked at the opposite end of the path. "I'm waiting for someone to help me with my bags."

"I can help."

Even at that age, little boys could be so disarmingly chivalrous. What a shame they had to grow up into dullards like her soon-to-be-husband. "I'm afraid they're too heavy for you, sweetheart."

"Can't you carry them yourself?"

She shook her head. "Afraid not."

"My daddy could carry both of them."

"Yes, well, I'm afraid your daddy isn't in the mood to help me right now."

"Kelse!" Lexi jumped at the sound of her intended's voice. "Come in and get your mittens!"

The child bounded off toward him looking for all the world like a frisky puppy. He couldn't be a total monster if his little boy was so crazy about him.

He strode down the path toward her looking like a gladiator in one of those old Tony Curtis-Kirk Douglas costume dramas she'd seen on TNT. Broad shoulders, muscular chest that tapered into a narrow waist and hips. His thighs—she felt her face flush. Not much point in thinking about those thighs. Those thighs were none of her business.

Even if she couldn't quite fathom how a bookworm ended up with thighs worthy of a lumberjack....

"This isn't getting us anywhere," he said without preamble.

She tilted her head and looked up at him. "I've noticed."

"Pretty cold out here."

"I've noticed that, too."

"You going to stay out here all night?"

"I've been considering it."

"I don't think either one of us has much say in this."

She frowned. "Freedom of choice doesn't exist in Alaska?"

He considered her for what seemed like a very long time. "I'll bring in your bags."

A huge smile spread across her face. "How wonderful of you." She turned back toward the house. "Just make sure you don't scuff the leather."

KIEL STARED after her in disbelief. She wasn't kidding. She didn't turn around and laugh or do anything to let him know she recognized the absurdity of her statement. The woman he'd been cursed with glided up the walkway as if it were a red carpet and she was the Queen of Sheba.

For the second time in less than an hour, he found himself contemplating murder.

"This isn't going to work," he muttered as he grabbed the suitcases and followed after her. If she made him that crazy in forty minutes, what would she be able to accomplish during an Alaskan winter?

Besides, what in hell were they thinking of at PAX headquarters? Either this dame had the brainpower of Einstein in a very intriguing package or one of their enemies had found the perfect way to blow his research to smithereens.

He chuckled grimly. Pretty apt metaphor, all things considered.

OF COURSE he didn't take all of the bags. He left her carry-on tote for her to drag into the house. She had packed two blow dryers, a set of steam rollers, her curling iron, three new skin creams especially formulated for cold weather, every eye shadow she owned, a new mascara, her electric toothbrush and ten extra pairs of her favorite brand of panty hose. She felt like she was dragging a Buick behind her.

The inside of the cabin was much nicer than Lexi had imagined. Except for the moosehead mounted on the far wall, it was actually rather agreeable. Lots of dark wood, overstuffed furniture and a huge fireplace. No wall display of beer cans or jockstraps hanging from the mantel the way she'd feared. While it lacked the sophisticated ambience of her Park Avenue apartment, it certainly was livable.

Whether or not she'd be able to live in it with the Incredible Hunk was anyone's guess.

"Come on," he said, heading toward a dimly lit hallway. "I want to get back to work."

"I'm not a pack mule," she muttered under her breath.

"What was that?" he asked over his shoulder.

"Nothing."

"You said you're not a pack mule."

If she could have lifted the tote bag, she would

have heaved it at his head. "If you heard me, why did you ask me to repeat it?"

"Because I hate being muttered at. If you have something to say, say it."

"From now on, your wish is my command," she said in a sweetly acid tone of voice.

"You don't do humble very well, do you?"

"I don't do humble at all."

She followed him into an average-size bedroom that was dominated by a king-size bed and a tiny chest of drawers.

He tossed her suitcases on the bed and gestured toward the closet. "I made room for your things."

She crossed the room and swung open the closet door. "Your clothes are still in here."

"I said I made room. I didn't say I evacuated."

"Why don't you put your clothes in your own closet?"

"This *is* my closet."

"What's *your* closet doing in *my* bedroom?"

He met her eyes. "You mean *our* bedroom."

She laughed out loud. "No, I don't."

"Yes, you do."

"You don't expect to sleep here, do you?"

"Yeah," he said. "Actually, I do."

"Absolutely not."

"Sorry, lady," he snapped, "but I'm not giving up my bed for anyone."

"Then I'll sleep in another bedroom."

"There isn't another bedroom."

She stared at the bed. It seemed to be getting

smaller by the second. The thought of sharing that tiny expanse of mattress with that enormous man made her feel faint. "Over my dead body."

His eyes brightened. "That can be arranged."

Chapter Three

"That does it!" Lexi stormed from the room in a blaze of righteous indignation. "If you think I have any intention of sharing a bed with you, you're sorely mistaken."

Kiel stormed right after her. "If you think I want to share a bed with you, lady, you need your head examined."

They stood in the middle of the front room and glared at each other.

"This is hopeless," Lexi said, wondering what he would do if she beaned him with the moose head. "I can't go through with it."

"I was thinking the same thing."

"We'll kill each other before the week is out."

His expression darkened. As if waiting that long were possible. "Maybe sooner."

"I'm going to call Joanna and tell her. I'm sure she can find someone else."

"The telephone is in the kitchen."

He certainly seemed in a hurry to put an end to this arrangement. Feeling slightly miffed, she found her way down the corridor to the kitchen. As kitchens went, it really wasn't that bad. She'd half expected a litter of dirty pots and pans stacked everywhere, but to her surprise the countertops were clear.

And clean. She ran a finger across the Formica backsplash over the sink. No dust. No mildew. No grunge. For the life of her, she couldn't imagine why he needed a wife.

Not that it was her problem any longer. She fumbled through her bag for her address book. It was buried under a mound of dry cleaners tickets, loose change and theater playbills. She chuckled hollowly. No more worrying about whether the dry cleaner would hold her red beaded gown until spring. With a little luck, she'd be home by this time tomorrow, jet-lagged and still looking for a husband.

''Sorry, Joanna,'' she murmured as she reached for the phone. ''Great idea. Wrong candidate.''

The telephone was one of those absurdly modern contraptions with all sorts of flashing lights and buttons that made the act of dialing a number into something akin to bringing the space shuttle in for a landing.

She pressed the button marked Line 1.

Nothing.

She pressed the button marked Line 2.

Still nothing.

Irritated, she jiggled the hook, banged the receiver against the edge of the counter, then proceeded to press every single button on the console with growing agitation.

Kiel burst into the room like a hand grenade. ''What the hell are you doing?''

"Trying to make a phone call," she snapped. "Don't you people up here believe in dial tones?"

"Give me that."

He grabbed the receiver from her, punched in a series of codes, then slammed the receiver back on the console. "Next time you have trouble with the phone, tell me. You could have—" He stopped abruptly.

"Could have what?" she asked, her curiosity sharpened.

"Daddy!" Kelsey pushed open the back door and trailed snow across the kitchen floor. "The whistles are blowing!" The child's eyes were wide with excitement.

"Nothing to worry about," Kiel said easily. "Lexi pushed the wrong button, that's all."

He sounded so cool, so calm, so *normal* that Lexi had a hard time reconciling the crazy man who'd screamed at her with the loving father.

"Your telephone sets off whistles?" she asked.

"It's an alarm system," he said as Kelsey went back outside to play.

"An alarm system?" She laughed despite herself. "What are you afraid of, a moose with a yen for a VCR?"

The look he gave her would have stopped a wiser woman in her tracks. "I don't give a damn about the VCR but I do give a damn about my kid."

"Of course you do," Lexi persisted despite the way a muscle in his jaw clenched and unclenched ominously. "But what are you protecting her from?"

He picked up the telephone, punched in yet another

code, then handed her the receiver. "Make your call."

She handed the receiver back to him. "There's no dial tone."

He held the receiver to his ear, muttered something rude, then fiddled with some switches on the side of the console. "No dial tone."

"That's what I said."

"The lines must be down between here and town."

"So now what?"

"We wait for them to go back up."

"But I want to get out of here."

"No more than I want you to," he said. A bit too heartily, in Lexi's opinion.

She gestured in the general direction of civilization. "Maybe one of your neighbors has phone service."

"I don't have any neighbors."

A chill ran up her spine. "There must be somebody."

"This is Alaska. Your next-door neighbor could be a hundred miles away."

She thought of six months alone in the tiny house with only Kiel Brown and his son for company. Six long winter months with two adults and one king-size bed. A dangerous combination. And, if she was honest with herself, especially dangerous when the man in question looked like Kiel.

Not that she was particularly attracted to him, mind you. It was just that his type usually assumed women would fall at his feet in adoration. Unfortunately for Mr. Brown, Lexi believed adoration was a one-way street with all the traffic heading in her direction.

Grown men had the habit of turning into quivering masses of protoplasm when they were around her. An odd reaction, perhaps, but one to which she'd become personally attached.

Mr. Tall-Dark-and-Ornery, however, barely seemed to notice she was female. She doubted if he even remembered the fact that they'd shared a kiss, a fact which made her feel more prickly and annoyed than it should.

Which, in turn, only made her dislike him all the more.

THEY STARED at each other for a good three minutes. Kiel wished he had a stopwatch because it was beginning to look like they might be going for an entry in the *Guiness Book of World Records.*

He had to hand it to her. She never blinked. Not once. Just leveled those baby blues on him and did her best to make him squirm.

Close call, pal, that little voice inside piped up. *You could've been stuck with her until the thaw.*

Just the two of them, sharing that king-size bed. Okay, they'd be sleeping in it at different times, but the thought was still enough to set his blood moving a little faster through his veins.

Which was exactly the way he didn't want to feel.

What in hell had PAX been thinking of when they sent this pint-size Mata Hari up here to take care of Kelsey? He'd expected a no-nonsense type, as brainy and single-minded as he was. She was single-minded, he'd give her that, and for all he knew, she had an advanced degree in quantum physics. His late wife had been beautiful and brainy. He knew one asset didn't negate the other. Still, Alexa Marsden wasn't exactly the kind of woman he envisioned digging her way through a foot of snow to get to the woodpile. She was the kind of woman who got other people to plow through the snow to get to the woodpile.

And as soon as the phones were back up, she'd be someone else's problem.

Connecticut

RYDER O'NEAL MET his wife's eyes across the conference table. "That's an old trick, Jo," he said with a shake of his head. "Cutting the phone lines."

"I'm wounded," she said. "Cutting the phone lines is a terribly outdated thing to do." A sly smile curved the ends of her mouth. "I had Larry in Communications jam them."

"Any particular reason?"

She pretended to scan some papers scattered in front of her. "Let's just call it woman's intuition."

"You make me nervous when you say things like that."

"After six years of marriage and two kids, you should be used to it."

"I know that look in your eye. What the hell are you up to?"

"Preventive maintenance," she said with a laugh calculated to make her husband even more nervous. "They've probably just had their first fight and they're looking for an escape hatch."

"And you want to make sure they can't find one."

"You know me too well."

His frown deepened. "You're not matchmaking, are you?"

She looked genuinely affronted. "How could you ask such a thing?" she countered. "Everyone knows Kiel isn't looking for romance."

"And we both know why Lexi was so eager to go off to Nowhere on a moment's notice."

"A terrible match," Joanna agreed.

"The worst," said her husband. "Lexi Marsden is a major pain in the butt."

"She's high-spirited."

"She was born with a silver spoon in her—"

"Watch it," Joanna warned. "She's my friend."

"I wouldn't wish her on my worst enemy."

"She's been at loose ends since her father died."

"She's been at loose ends since the day she was born. Being married to Lexi Marsden would be like being staked to an anthill."

Joanna took a deep breath and counted to ten. "Kiel needed a wife. Lexi needed a husband. She'd already been vetted by PAX the time we invited her up for the weekend and she's as politically unaffiliated as they come. Besides, who expected the situation in Eastern Europe to reach the flash point just when your absentminded professor decided he needed a wife."

"There had to be someone better, someone more professional."

"There isn't," said Joanna, struggling with her temper. "We're in Code 7 Alert Status. We can't afford to send any of our operatives up to Alaska. It's Lexi or nothing.''

He looked dubious. ''And you really think this is going to work?''

She nodded. ''I really do.''

''So when are you going to unjam the phone lines?''

''Soon.'' She looked down at her papers to hide her smile. ''Soon.''

IF IT HADN'T BEEN for Kelsey, Lexi and Kiel might have lived out the rest of their natural lives locked in eye-to-eye combat. *Thank God for children,* Lexi thought as the little boy burst through the back door, dragging something gray and disgusting behind him. An amazing thought but heartfelt.

''Daddy! Look what I found!''

Kiel's eyebrows slid together in a frown. ''Where did you find it?''

Kelsey looked sheepish and mumbled something.

''What was that?'' Kiel asked.

''...your house...'' Lexi heard the child say.

Kiel crouched down in front of his offspring. ''What did I tell you about playing near the lab?''

''You told me no.''

''And why did I tell you no?''

The little boy looked down at the floor. ''I could get hurt.''

''I want you to go to your room and think about that.''

Kelsey looked back up at his father. ''I don't wanna.''

"You're going anyway," said Kiel.

Lexi cleared her throat. "Aren't you being a little tough on Kelsey?"

Two dark heads swiveled in her direction. They looked as surprised by her words as she was.

"What was that?" Kiel asked in an ominous tone of voice.

She sighed loudly. "Forget I said anything." Far be it from Lexi to meddle in parental affairs.

He waited until Kelsey stomped off to his room before he lit into her.

"I don't need your advice on how to raise my kid."

She arched an eyebrow. "Oh really? You could've fooled me."

"What the hell does that mean?"

"That should be obvious. You were willing to marry me sight unseen to get a built-in baby-sitter."

The phrase "if looks could kill" suddenly took on new meaning. "Trust me, lady, it wasn't my idea."

"It wasn't my idea, either." Which was technically true if she wanted to lay the blame on her father and that ridiculous provision in his will. "You're not the friendliest man I've ever met."

"I'm not paid to be friendly."

"And I'm not paid to keep my mouth shut." Actually, she wasn't being paid anything at all, which was one of the reasons she was in the mess she was in. "I'm as much a victim in this as you are."

A VICTIM?

She was calling herself a victim?

Kiel couldn't help it. He started to laugh.

"How dare you laugh at me!" she said.

He couldn't have stopped if he wanted to—which he didn't. He couldn't remember the last time he'd laughed like this. Full-bodied. Loud. From the gut.

"Stop that!" she ordered, advancing on him with a murderous glint in her big blue eyes. "I refuse to stand here and be insulted!"

Still laughing, he pulled out a chair and gestured toward her.

She looked at the chair. Then back at him. Her tiny hands balled into fists. The thought of that fluffy piece of female outrage pummeling him made him laugh even louder.

"Damn good thing we're not getting married," he said when he found his composure again. "We'd kill each other before we made it to *I do.*"

Her eyes widened. He watched, fascinated, as the corners of her lush mouth twitched then stretched wide in a smile.

A real one.

One that even reached her eyes.

Suddenly he remembered the way her mouth had felt beneath his, all warm and soft and yielding. The harder he tried to banish the memory, the more real it became. Exactly what he wanted to avoid.

She glanced at the phone. "How long do you think it will be until the line is back up?"

"Don't worry about it," he said, feeling suddenly magnanimous. "You'll be out of here before nightfall."

"I can stand it that long if you can." She considered him for a moment, then extended her right hand. "Truce?"

"Yeah," he said as his hand enveloped hers. "I think we can manage it for an hour or two."

She arched an eyebrow. "I thought we'd take it on a minute-by-minute basis." The twinkle in her eyes softened the words.

He found himself grinning back at her. Now that he knew they wouldn't be stuck with each other through an Alaskan winter, he was feeling optimistic. "Hungry?"

She nodded. "Actually, I am."

"How does tomato soup sound?"

"Boring," she said, "but it will do."

His temper flared momentarily but he tamped it down. "Did you really think you were going to be eating caviar and bonbons up here?"

She sat down at the kitchen table, propping her elbows on the scarred wooden surface. "I didn't have time to think about it at all. When Jo called—" She stopped abruptly and looked away.

She must be new at this, Kiel thought as he rummaged through the pantry for a can of soup. Most agents scrupulously avoided any and all allusions to the organization when they were on an assignment.

Trouble was he couldn't even ask her. PAX maintained its security on a need-to-know basis. Ryder had told him that Alexa Marsden—a fake name if he'd ever heard one—would be told the same environmentalist story that Kiel had told everyone else in Nowhere and it was understood that any operative worth her salt would keep questions to herself.

You never knew what would trip you up in this business. Especially with a four-year-old girl added to the already-volatile mix.

Take care of yourself, sweetheart, he thought as he hooked the opener over the lip of the can. *Slip up one time too often and you'll find yourself dead.*

Even he knew it was an unforgiving business and he only worked on the fringes of the operation. Research scientists rarely found themselves in the middle of an intrigue—no matter how risky the science they're researching might be. He glanced over at Lexi. She was flipping through the issue of *Time* magazine he'd been reading over breakfast, seemingly absorbed in the minutiae of the current world situation.

He tried to imagine her slipping across international boundaries, smuggling important papers and risking her life to keep the world free for the spread of democracy.

The idea was laughable.

She turned the page with a languid, graceful motion that made him think of drawing rooms in English manor houses. He dumped the tomato soup into a pot, then took a container of milk from the fridge. She wasn't the guns-and-bullets type at all. No, PAX would have found better, more interesting ways to use a woman who looked like that. He had a brief flash of Ms. Marsden in the arms of a strapping freedom fighter from some war-torn eastern European battleground.

Whoa! He'd splattered milk all over the top of the stove. *Get a grip, man. What she does is none of your business.*

LEXI GRINNED and looked back down at the magazine she'd been perusing. He was clumsy. Strange, but she found that quality rather charming. Up until that moment, she'd half believed he was some kind of android straight out of an episode of "Star Trek." Mr. Perfect, with the muscular torso of a flashy film star and the laser-sharp brain of a computer.

When he made to pour the milk into the pot with the tomato soup, he missed it by a country mile and Lexi was pleased to note that she was the reason. An odd sensation filled her body, not unlike the sensation she'd experienced when he'd pulled her into his arms and claimed her mouth with his. There'd been something more than curiosity in his scrutiny, something very male, very primal.

It was nice to know that he wasn't immune to her, after all.

Not that she cared what Kiel Brown thought, mind you. It was just that a woman liked to know she wasn't losing her touch at the advanced age of twenty-four and a half.

"How old are you?" she asked, looking up from *Time*.

"Thirty-four." He tossed a dishrag into the sink then wiped his hands on a paper towel. "You taking a census or something?"

"Just curious. We were going to be married, after all."

He lit a fire under the pot of soup. "So how old are you?"

"Almost twenty-five."

"Most women wouldn't sound so eager to hit the quarter-century mark."

She thought of her inheritance. "Let's just say turning twenty-five has its compensations." She tossed the magazine aside and focused her full attention on him. "How long have you been an environmentalist?"

"You must be great at cocktail parties," he observed. "Are we playing Twenty Questions?"

"I'm being polite," she said, bristling. "Something you obviously know nothing about."

He leaned against the counter and crossed his arms over his chest. The effect was alarmingly powerful. She wondered if he knew exactly how powerful. *More than likely,* she thought as his biceps seemed to flex of their own volition. You didn't look at a body like that in the mirror every day of your life and not realize the impact it had on the opposite sex.

She, of course, was immune to his appeal.

"Do you want soup or not?" he asked.

Her stomach growled impolitely. "A little."

He shot her a look, then reached for an enormous white stoneware bowl that rested on an open shelf above the stove. He filled it, dropped in a spoon, then placed it on the table before her.

"This is too much," she said, appalled at the gallon of soup sloshing in front of her.

"You'll need it," he said, tossing a packet of crackers down next to her bowl. "Who knows when you'll catch another meal."

"You're logical," she said, lifting her spoon to her lips. "I've always hated that in a man."

He flipped a chair around and straddled it. "What else do you hate in a man?"

"Questions like that, for one." She swallowed the soup. "This could use a splash of sherry."

"I'll pass that on to the chef." He ripped open the packet and helped himself to a handful of crackers.

"You're spilling crumbs all over the table."

"My table," he pointed out with another maddening display of logic.

She gestured toward the stove. "Aren't you having soup?"

"I hate soup."

"What about Kelsey?"

"Finished before you got here."

She had nothing to say about that. She'd already learned he had a low flash point when it came to criticism of how he disciplined his child. Silence seemed the better part of valor.

After a few moments of silence, punctuated by the sound of her soup spoon returning repeatedly to the bowl, he got up and disappeared down the hall. Lexi let out a huge sigh of relief. His intensity was a bit daunting. He'd been watching her eat as if she were a new specimen on the endangered list. The thought of being the focus of that intensity on a twenty-four-hour basis made her feel faint.

He's a widower, Joanna had said when she proposed the idea to Lexi. *Helena was a physicist with an IQ even higher than Kiel's.*

Yes, Lexi had said, *but what did she look like?*

Joanna had just laughed off Lexi's question. The

truth was, Lexi knew exactly what the late Dr. Helena Worthington-Brown had looked like.

"Homely," she muttered into her soup. Most gorgeous men married mousy women. Lexi had a theory that preternaturally handsome men didn't much like sharing the spotlight...or the mirror. A brainy woman didn't pose half the threat a beautiful woman posed.

No wonder he'd disliked her on sight.

The knowledge didn't make Lexi like him any better, but it did explain away the total absence of romantic spark.

All of which would have made the situation absolutely perfect for her needs, except for the fact that they couldn't say two words to each other without getting into a scrap.

It won't be much longer, she thought as she crumbled two crackers into her soup, then quickly gobbled up the evidence. Telephone troubles or no telephone troubles, she'd be on her way home before nightfall or know the reason why.

Chapter Four

By 4:00 p.m., it was apparent to both Lexi and Kiel that she wasn't going anywhere. At least not tonight.

"Damn phone," said Kiel, slamming the receiver down in the cradle. "It's never done this before."

She looked up at him from the rocking chair near the fireplace. "I thought you said this happens all the time."

"Never lasted this long."

"You don't have one of those cellular phones, do you? A car phone maybe."

"You sound desperate," he said, giving her a curious look.

"Not yet," said Lexi with a groan. "You'll know I'm desperate when I suggest smoke signals."

"It won't come to that."

"How do you know?" she demanded. "So far you haven't been right about anything."

"Believe me, I want you out of here as much as you do."

To Lexi's horror, her cheeks suddenly flamed with color. "That's impossible," she said, wishing her voice didn't sound quite so vulnerable. "If I had a sense of direction, I'd start walking."

"Good idea," he said, poking the fire with a particularly nasty-looking stick. "You'd make a great appetizer for a hungry bear."

"Very funny." She pulled her jacket more closely around her. "I bet you say that to all your ex-fiancées."

"I'm not kidding," he persisted. "We see bear every few weeks around here."

"I really don't want to hear this."

"If you're thinking of going for an after-dinner walk tonight, you'd better hear it."

Bear, thought Lexi. Big deal. If he was trying to make her feel inadequate, he was failing miserably. Besides, what made him think he was such a bargain?

"Can you use a microwave?"

She looked at him. "What?"

"A microwave," he repeated.

"Of course I can use a microwave."

"Great," he said, grabbing his jacket from the peg by the front door. "There's a beef stew in the freezer. Kelsey gets a glass of milk with dinner."

"Where do you think you're going?"

"To work," he said. "As long as you're going to be here tonight, I might as well get something done."

"And leave me here alone?"

"It's not like we're enjoying each other's company, is it?"

"No, but—"

"Exactly. Help yourself to anything you want. Kelse will show you where everything is."

"You're just going to walk out on me?"

He opened the front door. "Buzz me on the intercom if the phone lines go back up."

And with that he was gone.

SHE SMELLED like lilacs. She wasn't supposed to smell like lilacs.

None of the women in Nowhere smelled like lilacs. Most of them smelled like soap and water and fresh air. All of which he appreciated but to which he was immune.

He wasn't immune to lilacs.

Her scent lingered in his nostrils as he stomped through the snow on his way to the small building that housed his lab. He had half a mind to stick his head in the first available snowbank in an attempt to bring his temperature back down to normal.

"Damn it," he muttered as he punched in five successive code numbers, then waited for the electronic security device to scan his fingerprint. Kissing her hadn't brought about the violent chemical chain reaction inside his body that the scent of lilacs in her hair had set in motion.

The buzzer sounded and he entered the lab, slamming the door shut behind him. The security devices whirred into action, executing a series of sophisticated locks and monitors.

Too bad there wasn't a device that could secure a man's libido.

It had been a long time since he'd made love to a woman. For months after Helena's death, he'd been too numb, both physically and emotionally, to think of sex. Kelsey was only two years old at the time, and her needs had far outstripped his own.

After a while, lust reentered his life.

He doubted if love ever would again.

The air in his lab was neutral. Moderately warm. Moderately dry. It was dust-free, germ-free, noise-free. The perfect, sterile environment for research that could change the future of the world.

And it didn't smell of lilacs.

At the moment, that was the most important thing of all to Kiel.

"NOT THAT BUTTON," said Kelsey an hour later. "First you press the big one, then you press the little one."

Four years old, Lexi reminded herself. *Remember, he's only four years old.* "Thank you," she said in a stiff and formal tone of voice that reminded her of one of the nannies she'd had when she was a little girl.

She pressed the big button, then the little one. Wouldn't you know it: the microwave came to life as if by magic.

She sat back down at the kitchen table and took a sip of some very bad wine she'd found in the closet that served as an ill-equipped pantry.

Kelsey looked at her over the top of a mug of milk. "I can make toast."

"So can I," said Lexi. *Good going, Alexa Grace. Trying to one-up a child.*

"I can butter it and add jam."

Lexi thought for a moment. "I can make cereal."

Kelsey laughed into his milk. "Silly. The store makes the cereal."

Lexi smiled broadly. Finally, a subject she could handle. "The store doesn't make the cereal," she countered, trying not to sound too smug. "The cereal factory makes the cereal."

"Then who makes the factory?"

"I don't know who makes the factory." She took another sip of wine.

"Somebody made it."

"I know that," said Lexi, "but I don't know who it was."

Kelsey leaned back in his chair. His eyes twinkled with mischievous glee. "The builder makes the factory."

Lexi considered her nemesis. "You're pretty smart for a four-year-old, aren't you?"

Kelsey nodded. "I'm a genius."

"You're not very modest."

"I don't know what that is."

At last! "A modest person doesn't tell everyone good things about himself. He waits for people to find out for themselves."

"But you said I was smart."

"You're right," Lexi agreed with a sigh. "I did say that." It was a bit like being trapped in the Lincoln Tunnel during rush hour with a talkative cab-driver who didn't speak English.

"You're pretty," said Kelsey.

Lexi's ears perked up. "Why, thank you." Nice to know one of the Browns felt that way.

Kelsey blew some bubbles in his mug of milk. "Are you going to live with us?"

"I don't think so, honey. I'm going home as soon as the phones are working."

The microwave dinged. She pushed back her chair and stood up. "Dinner's ready."

Kelsey nodded. "I want my blue bowl."

"Okay," said Lexi. She rummaged through the cupboard over the stove until she found a turquoise bowl with white-and-yellow flowers painted along the border. Not at all what she'd expected. She turned toward the boy. "Is this it?"

"My mommy got that before I was born."

Oh, please, thought Lexi as she moved the step stool back into the corner where she'd found it. *I don't think I can handle this.* What on earth did you say to a child who'd lost his mother in a tragic accident? Lexi remembered the foolish things people had said to her when her own mother had died just before Lexi's sixth birthday. Better to say nothing, she decided.

She popped open the microwave, then reached for the Tupperware container filled with stew. "Ouch!" She leaped back, waving her hands in the air madly.

"Pot holders," Kelsey said sagely. "Daddy uses pot holders."

"You could have told me that," Lexi said, running her fingers under cold water. "That bowl's hot!"

"Didn't anyone ever tell you about pot holders?"

"No," Lexi snapped. "No one ever told me that."

"But how do you make your food at home?"

"I don't make my food at home. Someone *else*

makes my food at home." *And once I get my inheritance, I'll never touch a microwave oven again as long as I live.*

"Your mommy?"

Lexi's throat tightened. That was so many years ago. You'd think she'd be over it by now. "Not my mother," she said carefully. "Someone who works for me." Rather, a series of someones, none of whom ever stayed very long.

"Do you work for my daddy?"

"Of course not!" Lexi ladled some stew into the child's bowl. She searched around for a nice soup plate for her own portion, then settled on a plain white dinner plate. "Napkins," she said, poking around in drawers and cupboards. "There must be some around here."

"There!"

Lexi turned to look at the child. "What?"

Kelsey pointed toward the sink. "The napkins are there."

Lexi glanced in that direction and saw nothing but a window and a roll of paper towels. "Napkins, honey, not paper towels."

"Daddy says they're better than napkins."

"They're paper," Lexi said, aghast. "Napkins are made of linen."

Kelsey frowned. "What's linn-inn?"

"Cloth," said Lexi. "Nice, tight-weave cloth that civilized people put on their laps at mealtime."

But apparently not in this house. With a shudder, Lexi ripped off two squares of paper toweling and carried them to the table. The selection of flatware wasn't much better but she at least found service for one that matched. Kelsey was content with a *Beauty and the Beast* spoon.

She took her seat opposite the child, placed the paper towel on her lap, then surveyed the scene. Kelsey had jammed the paper towel into the neckline of his shirt. Lexi decided to ignore it. There was something else that irritated her more.

''No G.I. Joe at the table,'' she said, pointing to the grubby doll lying near Kelsey's mug of milk.

Kelsey took a bite of stew.

''Kelsey.'' Lexi's voice rose a tad. ''Dolls don't belong on the table.'' *Especially not dolls that look as if they could have won Desert Storm single-handedly.*

The child chewed and swallowed.

Lexi waited a moment, then leaned over and grabbed G.I. Joe by the bullet clip. In a moment of inspiration, she sat him down on the empty chair to her right.

Kelsey looked at her, then at the doll.

Lexi waited for the explosion.

But there wasn't one.

Kelsey returned to the stew with renewed interest. G.I. Joe minded his own business. The Incredible Hunk stayed in his lab.

Lexi glanced at her watch. The day was almost over. She was still alive, she still had her sanity.

Only one hundred and eighty-seven more days like this one and she'd have her inheritance, to boot.

It was enough to make a woman stop and rethink.

Connecticut

"Now?" asked the technician, hand poised over the keypad.

Joanna checked her watch, then nodded. "Now."

Ryder watched from the far corner of the room. "Something's going to go wrong," he said in ominous tones. "I can feel it."

"Nothing's going to go wrong," his wife said, glancing at him over her shoulder. "Besides, if Kiel had wanted to reach us badly enough, he has other ways."

"They've probably killed each other by now."

"Maybe not," said Joanna.

"You don't sound very convinced."

"You're being ridiculous," Joanna said. "They're both intelligent, highly motivated human beings. They'll make the best of the situation."

Ryder's response was unprintable.

"Nice talk for the father of two," Joanna said dryly. "If I remember right, you didn't have much choice in the matter."

The technician leaned back in her chair. "Done, boss," she said to Joanna. "System's back up and running."

"Thanks, Sharon."

"Anything else?"

Joanna shook her head. "You can go back to what you were doing."

Ryder waited until the technician closed the door behind her. "What if something goes wrong?" he asked his wife. "There might be movement in their area. She's not trained to do anything but shop."

"She's a smart woman," Joanna said. "A hell of a lot smarter than you think. Besides, she's there to take care of Kelsey, not save the world."

"Yeah," said Ryder. "Let's hope it stays that way."

WHO WAS he kidding?

Kiel powered down his equipment and turned off his computer.

He hadn't accomplished one damn thing since he locked himself in his lab four hours ago. He'd been trying so hard to forget about what was going on in the house that he'd been unable to think of anything but Lexi Marsden.

She had the disposition of a rattlesnake.

The sleek line of her thighs as she sat in the rocking chair.

She thought technology had peaked with the invention of the blow dryer and the lighted makeup mirror.

The way the firelight made her pale blond hair glow.

She turned every verbal exchange between them into a major battle of wills.

The scent of lilacs that continued to haunt him.

He groaned and dragged a hand through his hair.

And she was the only game in town. He knew the powers-that-be well enough to know they'd sent her here for a reason. She had to have some underlying value, some talent or gift that was invisible to the naked eye. And he also knew they weren't going to let her turn her back on the assignment without a damn good reason.

"You're going to have to learn to live with her," he said aloud in the silent laboratory. His work demanded a total commitment, something that was impossible without someone to care for Kelsey.

He knew the clock was ticking on his research work. With the breakup of the Soviet Union, nuclear warheads had become a hot commodity on the black market and every little country with ready cash was eager to arm itself to the teeth. Democratization was taking its toll, in ways the world could not have foreseen. It used to be arms for hostages. Now it was arms for bread as starving nations struggled to feed their people while they learned to live with independence.

Hard to believe it was only a year ago that PAX had plucked him out of his Boston Brain Trust and spirited him into the world of spies and counterespionage and terrorist plots.

The research he was working on could change the world for the better. He was close—so close—to a breakthrough that sometimes he couldn't sleep because his mind kept replaying the formulas, turning them around, trying to find the last piece of the puzzle. The ability to disable active warheads and neutralize the resultant nuclear waste was beyond comprehension.

But it could be done.

And he intended to be the one who did it.

He pushed back his chair and stood up. They'd gotten off to a bad start, that was all. They didn't have to like each other just because they were supposed to get married. Hell, they didn't even have to talk to each other if they didn't want to. He'd provide everything she needed to live a pleasant life. All she had to do was make sure his daughter was safe and happy.

We can do it, he thought as he locked up the laboratory and set the alarms. They were two adults, after all. Two adults who understood responsibility and reality and the importance of working as a team.

And it wasn't all her fault.

He'd been every bit as obnoxious himself. It wouldn't have killed him to carry all of her bags inside. Just because they were working together didn't mean he had to forget what little he knew about polite behavior.

Besides, there wasn't time to find someone else. He needed to string together some eighteen-hour days and he needed to start now. The only way that was going to happen was if he and Alexa Grace Marsden found a way to make it happen.

"Okay," he said as he started across the snow-covered field to the house. "This can work." It would take some effort on both of their parts but it could be done. He'd go in there and talk to her and no matter how annoying she was, he'd hold his temper. And he wouldn't notice the lilacs.

He pushed open the front door and a wave of warmth enveloped him. He grinned as he hung his jacket on the peg by the door. She knew how to keep the fire blazing in the hearth. Not a bad skill to have if you're going to spend the winter in Alaska.

"Alexa!" His voice rang out in the empty room. "We need to talk."

No repsonse.

"Alexa!" Louder this time. He tried not to think of all the things that could have gone wrong while he was holed up in the lab. "Where are you?"

"In the bathroom," she called out. "I'm helping Kelsey undress." And then, "Oh my God!" Her shriek pierced the air.

His imagination raced out of control.

Broken glass under tiny feet.

Fractured skull.

Blood everywhere.

He tore into the bathroom and found Kelsey naked as the day she was born. She stood in the middle of the bathtub, wailing loud enough to wake the dead. Her little face was contorted with tears but she looked hale and whole. No bruises, no cuts, no broken bones. Relief blasted through him and came close to buckling his knees.

Wrapping his daughter in a big fluffy bath towel, he scooped her out of the tub and held her against his chest. "What's wrong, Kelsey?" he asked, stroking her wet hair. "What happened?"

"He's a girl."

He spun around to see Lexi sitting on the closed toilet seat. "What did you say?"

She pointed toward his daughter. "He's a girl."

At that Kelsey wailed louder. "What in hell did you think she was, a cocker spaniel?"

"They told me she was a girl but I thought they'd made a mistake."

"You need help," he said, shaking his head. "You can't tell a girl from a boy."

That dangerous sparkle was back in her eyes. "Obviously I had no trouble once she got into the bathtub," she snapped, "but before that it was a tad difficult."

He leaned back and took a good look at his child. Big blue eyes, long lashes, a tiny and determined chin. "You're blind."

"The child was wearing baggy jeans and a baseball cap. What was I supposed to think?"

"That she's a normal kid," he roared.

"Look at her hair," Lexi said, gesturing toward Kelsey. "When was the last time you had it styled?"

"She's four years old, dammit. You want her sitting under a dryer in some ridiculous beauty parlor?"

"Nobody said anything about sitting her under a hair dryer." The woman was amazingly persistent. In a weird way, he admired her for it. "I'm saying she's a little girl. She deserves more than a pair of old jeans and a baseball cap."

"If a man said that, you'd call him a sexist pig."

She shook her head. "I'd say he cared about his little girl."

"What planet are you from, anyway?" he exploded as Kelsey, tears drying on her cheeks, listened to the exchange. "These are the nineties. Little girls are more than sugar and spice."

"And they're more than G.I. Joe and high-top sneakers."

"I want a dress like Beauty wore when she danced with the Beast."

Kiel felt as if he'd been kicked in the solar plexus. He stared at Kelsey as if she were an alien. "What?"

Kelsey's eyes took on a dreamy expression. "A yellow dress," she went on, glancing shyly at Lexi, "with a big fat skirt."

Lexi's smile was triumphant. "What did I tell you?" Her smile grew even more triumphant. "Kelsey knows what I'm talking about even if her father doesn't."

Kiel's eyebrows knotted. "You want a fancy yellow dress?" he asked Kelsey.

She nodded vigorously. "And a machine gun for G.I. Joe."

He hugged his daughter tighter and started to laugh.

"That tickles!" Kelsey pushed at his chin with both hands.

Still smiling, he met Lexi's eyes across the top of his daughter's head. To his amazement, she smiled back at him.

"We need to talk," she said, sounding more approachable than she'd sounded since her arrival.

He nodded. "After I put Kelsey down for the night."

"You must be hungry," Lexi said. "I'll heat up the rest of the stew."

"Pot holders," said Kelsey.

Kiel glanced down at his daughter. "What?"

"Girl talk," said Lexi, heading toward the door. "I'll see to the stew."

Kiel stared after her. "I don't get it," he said aloud. "One minute she's Princess Di, the next she's Old

Mother Hubbard. What gives?'' He ruffled his little girl's hair. ''Do you know, Kelse?''

Kelsey nodded. ''She's pretty,'' said his daughter, ''but she doesn't know about pot holders.''

Which summed up Alexa Grace Marsden about as well as anything could.

THE MICROWAVE beeped twice. Lexi popped open the door and reached for the container of beef stew.

''Pot holders,'' she said, jumping back at the first touch of heat against her fingertips. *From the mouths of babes...*

To her amazement, Lexi found herself smiling as she thought of Kelsey. Admittedly, it had been a shock to discover that Kiel Brown's scruffy little boy was really a scruffy little girl, and Lexi wished she'd managed to stifle her scream of surprise when she first realized that fact. Poor Kelsey probably thought she was mad as a hatter.

And maybe she was.

''I can do this,'' she said as she set a place for Kiel at the kitchen table, then sat down to nurse a cup of coffee. It had been a long day. She'd traveled thousands of miles, left everything she knew behind and found herself in the middle of a ready-made family. No wonder she felt short-tempered and overwhelmed.

Once she got the hang of it, she was certain she and Kelsey would get on together just fine. Besides, it wouldn't hurt the child to have a feminine influence around, even if it was only for six months. Kelsey was a cute little thing, if a bit rough around the edges, and Lexi had no doubt she'd be even cuter once Lexi got to work.

THERE WAS SOMETHING about the sight of a beautiful woman sitting at the kitchen table that awakened the cave dweller in a man.

The fact that he'd followed the scent of lilacs all the way down the hall didn't help matters any. Not even the robust aroma of beef stew could compete.

Kiel stood in the doorway and let the scene wash over him. She'd set a place for him at the table, complete with a square of paper towel folded into a fan shape and tucked with a flourish into his water glass. Curls of steam rose from the ironstone bowl. She sat opposite his chair, her pointed chin resting in her highly incapable-looking hands. Her eyes were closed; the thick tangle of lashes cast a shadow against the curve of her cheekbones.

She was so damn small, so finely made. He had no doubt he could span her waist with his hands. His breath snagged deep in his throat and for a moment he imagined he could feel the supple curve beneath his fingers as he moved his hands up over her rib cage until the gentle swell of her breasts filled his palms and—

"Oh!" She started, eyes fluttering open as she grew suddenly aware of his presence. "I must have been daydreaming."

He found himself grinning easily as he took his seat. "Sleeping's more like it."

"I wasn't sleeping," she said, that backbone of steel reasserting itself. "Just resting my eyes."

"Right," he said, reaching for his fork. "Whatever you say."

She stifled a yawn. "Well, maybe I am a little tired. Back home it's almost midnight."

He started shoveling in the stew, then stopped abruptly at the look of horror on her face. "Something wrong?" he asked, wiping his mouth with the intricately folded square of paper towel.

"Your table manners," she said.

He speared a cube of beef. "What about 'em?"

"They're nonexistent."

He chewed, then swallowed. "Never had any complaints before."

"Obviously you've been away from civilization for a while."

"Don't tell me," he said. "You're one of those charm-school graduates who thinks the meaning to life can be found written on the back of a lace doily."

Something suspiciously close to a giggle broke through her stern demeanor. "There's nothing foolish about dining in a civilized manner," she said. "Especially not when you have a daughter looking to you for guidance."

"Kelsey's table manners aren't so bad."

"Compared to whose?" she retorted. "Yours?"

"I'm doing the best I can, lady. It's not easy being mother, father, teacher and nu—" He caught himself in the nick of time. He'd almost said *nuclear physicist.* "And environmental scientist."

She didn't bat an eye. He'd never realized what a cool liar he could be.

"I know it's hard," she said smoothly. "And that's why I'm staying."

Chapter Five

He didn't say anything. Lexi took that as a good sign and plunged ahead. "I thought about it while you were in your lab counting birds. We're both adults. We understand the rules. We don't have to like each other in order to live together. You need someone to take care of your daughter and I need—" She stopped. It wouldn't do to say she needed a temporary husband so she could collect some very permanent money. Men, even men who didn't particularly like you, could be very sensitive about things like that.

"Go ahead," he said, leaning back in his chair and watching her with those devastating blue eyes of his. "What do you need?"

You, she thought, then felt herself flush deep red with embarrassment. Where on earth had such a ridiculous notion come from? The last thing on earth she wanted was to be mixed up with a man like Kiel Brown. He might be brilliant, she'd grant him that, but she liked her men polished and sophisticated and polite. Everything Kiel Brown wasn't.

"I'm waiting," he said, still watching her closely. "Tell me what you need, Alexa Grace."

Even the way he said her name was wrong. Somehow he made it sound like a caress, a long, slow voluptuous rise and fall of vowels and consonants that made her shiver. "I need this assignment," she said finally, recovering her poise. "I came here to take care of your daughter and I intend to honor that commitment."

"Not if I don't want you to."

Wonderful, she thought angrily. He was going to make her beg. "You need me as much as I need this assignment."

The fiery glitter in his eyes turned to ice. "I'll tell this to you once," he said, his voice as cold as the winds buffeting the cabin. "I don't need anyone."

She thought of the little girl asleep in the other room. "You don't mean that."

"You know what I'm talking about," he snapped. "If we go through with this, it's a marriage in name only."

"Of course," said Lexi, highly affronted that he would even suggest she'd consider him a worthy romantic partner. "A business arrangement."

He leaned forward again, gesturing with his fork. "If there was another way to do this without getting married, I'd do it."

"Naturally," said Lexi, thanking her lucky stars that there wasn't another way. "You certainly don't think I'm looking forward to a marriage of convenience, do you?"

"Marriage is a lot of things," Kiel said. "Convenient isn't one of them."

A bad marriage, she thought suddenly. So he and

his wife weren't the match-made-in-heaven that Joanna had thought they'd been. She reached for her cup of coffee and took a sip, trying to look nonchalant. "So when is the wedding?"

"Wedding?" He made it sound like a four-letter word. "There won't be a wedding."

"Wait just a minute," she said, slamming her coffee cup back down on the table. "I thought—"

"If you're looking for hearts and flowers, forget it," he broke in. "We're driving up to Black Wolf Pass tomorrow morning. The circuit judge will take care of everything."

"Great," said Lexi.

"Yeah," said Kiel. "Great."

AFTER SUPPER Kiel poured himself a thermos of coffee, then walked back across the moonlit yard to his laboratory. Overhead, the northern lights wove their magical spell and, for the first time since he'd arrived in Alaska, he didn't notice.

All he could think of was Alexa Grace Marsden.

"You're a damn fool," he muttered as he locked the lab door behind him, then hung his jacket up on the peg. There she was, nothing but trouble in a five-foot-two package of dynamite, and he was about to take her as his wife.

He could have sent her back. The phones were working again. He'd tried them right after he put Kelsey down for the night. Punch in a code, punch in PAX's number, and he could have told Ryder O'Neal to bag the whole damn idea and send him a seventy-five-year old housekeeper instead. Let her pose as his

for all he cared, but get Lexi out of his
ast.

ny didn't you?'' he asked the four walls as
d the length of his laboratory. Being direct
ever been one of his problems. He usually said
he thought, consequences be damned. It was one
the many traits that made him better off alone in
research lab and not saddled with some political
patronage gig where charm was more important than
ains.

tting rid of a hot-tempered blonde with an atti-
oblem should have been as easy as brushing
And a hell of a lot more enjoyable. God
knows, ...d made it clear that the situation was
equally untenable from her vantage point. She didn't
like the town, the house, the sleeping arrangements, Kelsey's fashion statement or his table manners. The last thing he'd expected was for her to say she intended to go through with the marriage.

No, he thought ruefully, that wasn't quite right. The last thing he'd expected was the sense of relief that flooded through him when she said she'd go through with the marriage. He wasn't supposed to feel that way. Hell, he wasn't supposed to feel anything at all. Not for her or anybody. Only Kelsey.

"Sex,'' he said aloud as he powered up the various computers and machines that were part and parcel of his work. "That's what it is.'' That primal urge to bury yourself in a woman, to spill your seed, to find release in the ancient order of things. It had been a long time and he was only human. Put a slab of meat

in front of a hungry bear and you didn
Einstein to figure out what happened next
He doubted if Alexa would find that ana
tering, but it got the point across. He was res
to her on a sexual level. His hormones were lin
like a row of penny arcade ducks just waiting
shot down. He grinned. She probably wouldn't
that analogy, either.

She was a woman.

He was a man.

It was only natural that that fact would get his blood racing.

That they didn't much like each other mattered with every minute that passed. You coul woman without liking her. And, damn wanted Alexa in every way possible.

Come tomorrow, it was going to be hard as hell to remember that in their case "I do" really meant "I don't."

THE DRIVE TO Black Wolf Pass took one hour and twenty minutes. Lexi knew that for a fact because Kelsey asked for a time update at least once every ten minutes.

"Gotta teach her to tell time," Kiel muttered as he maneuvered the Jeep through a series of hairpin curves.

Lexi said nothing. She couldn't have said anything if she wanted to. The lump in her throat seemed to grow bigger the closer they got to Black Wolf Pass and Judge Moreland.

They were getting married.

The enormity of it all hit her right between the eyes. Was it any wonder she'd been awake all night, curled up in a corner of the couch, thinking about all that lay ahead?

It didn't matter that it was a marriage of convenience, a business arrangement. The truth was that in a little while they would take their vows and Judge Moreland would pronounce them husband and wife and they'd be married the way her parents had been married and her grandparents and everyone else who'd ever loved enough to pledge their lives to one another.

It made a woman stop and think.

Of course, thinking was the one thing Lexi didn't want to do. Thinking was how she got that lump in her throat in the first place. She was supposed to turn off her brain, smile brightly, and say "I do." All of which had sounded much easier than it was turning out to be.

"Are we almost there yet?" she asked Kiel, unable to suppress the question.

He glanced at her, then back at the road. "You, too? You sound like Kelse."

"Really," she persisted. "How much longer?"

They crested a hill and he pointed toward a small, low building to the right. "About thirty seconds," he said. "That's the courthouse."

"Oh God...." She closed her eyes for a moment, trying to summon up her resolve. *This is all your fault, Daddy.* she thought. *Why couldn't you just leave a normal inheritance like every other father on earth?*

And Joanna O'Neal shared some of the blame as

well. Joanna knew her situation. She knew Lexi wasn't looking for romance or commitment. All she was looking for was a husband. Wouldn't you think her friend would have found her a man who was a little less…manly than the one she was about to marry? A little less gorgeous would have been nice…a little less arrogant…a little less of just about everything.

But no matter. There wasn't time to quibble. Kiel pulled up in front of the building, turned off the engine, then met her eyes. "Next stop, matrimony."

"Very funny," she said. "Especially in front of Kelsey."

"Am I getting married, too?" Kelsey asked as she and G.I. Joe climbed out of the truck.

"Not for about thirty years," said Kiel, taking her hand in his.

"You don't think much of the institution, do you?" Lexi remarked as they walked up the path to the front door.

"I don't think of the institution at all," he said. "Do you?"

Lexi gave a "who, me?" type of shrug. "It's never been one of my priorities."

They were ushered inside by a plain-faced woman in tan corduroy trousers and a red plaid flannel shirt. "Fred will be with you in a moment." She retrieved some papers from a utilitarian file cabinet in the corner of the front room. "I'll need you both to sign these papers."

Kiel signed quickly. He had a sprawling hand, not at all what she expected from a tidy research type.

But then, why should that surprise her? Nothing about him was at all what she'd expected. Why should his handwriting be any different?

He handed her the pen. She took a deep breath and signed "Alexa Grace Mars—" She looked up. "Do I sign Marsden or Brown?"

The woman in red flannel smiled at her. "Maiden name now," she said. "Married name after the ceremony."

Lexi nodded, signed, then handed the document to the woman.

Kelsey tugged at the hem of her coat. She wore a bright blue sweater, a white down jacket, and her hair was caught up into two lopsided ponytails. Lexi itched to take a brush to the little girl's hair but there wasn't time.

"Will you be my mommy now?" Kelsey asked.

Lexi looked at Kiel but he said nothing.

"I'm going to take care of you, if that's what you mean."

Kelsey shook her head. "No. Will you be my mommy?"

The lump in Lexi's throat returned. "I—I suppose I will." Dear God. Why had she never thought of it that way before?

A tall man in an outfit uncannily like his assistant's strode into the room. "Kiel." The man shook Kiel's hand. "Alexa." Her own hand disappeared into the man's clasp. "I'm Fred Moreland." He bent down and extended a hand to Kelsey who stared up at him with curiosity. He straightened up. "If you're ready, we can perform the ceremony in my office."

Kiel and Lexi nodded. Kelsey clasped G.I. Joe close to her chest.

They followed Judge Moreland into his office.

And three minutes later, they followed him back out again.

"Good luck to you," said Judge Moreland, shaking their hands once again.

His assistant Marta dabbed at her eyes with a pink handkerchief. "I just love weddings," she said, sniffing loudly.

"I can't believe it," said Lexi as they climbed back into the Jeep. "It was over so fast."

"What did you expect?" Kiel asked as he started the engine. "A twenty-one-gun salute?"

"I don't know what I expected," Lexi said, "but it takes me longer to put on my mascara every morning."

"What's mass-kaa-ruh?" asked Kelsey from the back seat.

"Eye paint," said Kiel, heading back toward Nowhere.

Lexi made a face. She turned around to look at Kelsey. "See my eyelashes?" Kelsey nodded. "Mascara is what makes them dark and curly."

Kelsey looked from Lexi to her doll. "Joe wears mass-kaa-ruh, too."

Kiel snorted with laughter. Lexi barely restrained the urge to kick him. Actually, it looked as though Joe wore lipstick as well, but kids these days were having enough trouble with gender identity. Why add any more fuel to the fire?

THEY RODE in silence for a good twenty miles. Kiel cast around for a neutral topic of conversation and rejected each one in turn. There was no point in talking about the wedding. Moreland was a nice enough guy but the whole thing had been a sorry exercise in legalities. He considered a conversation about the weather but it was cold and clear and uneventful. Not the stuff of which witty dialogue was made. They could have talked about Kelsey but not with his inquisitive little daughter in the car. And they couldn't talk about PAX.

Which pretty much left them silent as two statues in Madame Tussaud's Wax Museum.

He cleared his throat about fifteen miles from home. "There's a roadhouse not too far from here," he said. "Thought we might grab some lunch."

"Pizza?" asked Kelsey.

"Maybe," he said, grinning at her in the rearview mirror. "What do you say, Alexa?"

"Whatever you like," she said primly.

"You don't look like the burgers-and-fries type."

"You're very perceptive."

"If you don't want to stop for lunch, just say so."

"I—" She stopped. He watched as your chin began to quiver, then her lower lip, then her entire face. A second later, she was crying into her gloved hands.

"What the hell?" He pulled over to the side of the road. "What's wrong?"

"N-nothing."

"You sick?"

"No."

"Does something hurt?"

"N-nothing hurts."

"Why the hell are you crying?"

She looked at him and wailed even louder. Kelsey leaned forward in her seat, her big blue eyes wide with curiosity. "Maybe she has a tummy ache."

Lexi shook her head. She didn't stop crying.

"Don't cry," said Kelsey, her own lower lip beginning to quiver in an alarming fashion. "We like you."

Speak for yourself, Kelse, he thought. Right now he would have welcomed the appearance of space aliens looking for an able-bodied earthling to take home as a specimen.

"Are you going to tell me what's wrong or do you expect me to guess?"

"It—it's our wedding day," she said. As if that explained everything.

"And?"

She glared at him. "If I have to tell you, then it doesn't matter."

"Is that supposed to make sense?"

"It would if you weren't such a barbarian."

"You're not getting sentimental on me, are you?" Where in hell did PAX find this one? Agents were supposed to have computer chips instead of hearts. Emotions were unheard of. And this woman was pure emotion.

"Excuse me," she said, sniffling. "This is the first time I've been married. How was I to know how it would feel?"

Good question. "All things considered," he said carefully, "I didn't think it would mean anything."

"Neither did I," she said.

"It shouldn't mean anything."

"I know it shouldn't. But when the judge said those words, I—" He watched, fascinated, as she struggled to regain control of her emotions. "I've probably played into every stereotype of the dumb blonde, haven't I?"

It was an easy opening. There were at least a half dozen one-liners he could have used against her. But he didn't. Something came over him, a desire to make her tears go away, and he offered up an easy smile instead. "Why don't we get some lunch? The roadhouse is usually filled with a few real Alaskan types. You might like it."

She shook her head. "I'd rather go home."

"Come on," he urged. "We might not have another chance."

She shook her head again. "I look dreadful," she said. She met his eyes. "We both know why we got married. Let's not make this situation any more confusing than it already is."

It occured to him that he could pull her into his arms and kiss away her tears.

It also occured to him that he could climb to the top of Denali and jump off.

Either way he'd be a dead man.

He headed for home.

IDIOT.

Fool.

Dope.

Of all the stupid, ridiculous things to do, bursting

into tears had to take the cake. If she had the nerve, she'd open the car door and leap out. She'd rather fend with asphalt burns and grizzly bears than the embarrassment of facing the man who was her husband after he'd seen her at her worst.

She'd never been the type of woman who cried at weddings. She was the only one of her set to sit through *Phantom of the Opera, Sommersby,* and *Beauty and the Beast* and not shed a single tear. Wouldn't you know she'd turn into a sentimental fool in front of her new husband.

For a second there, she'd actually thought he wanted to kiss her. His eyes had dropped to her mouth. An awareness of some primal pull…some indefinable chemistry.

She stifled a groan. Now she was really acting like an idiot. If she really believed he was interested in her sexually, she would leap out of the car and take her chances with that grizzly. He could overpower a woman, her husband could. The sheer size of him, the force of his will. He could take what he wanted, consequences be damned, and what woman would be strong enough to stop him? Alone in a cabin in the middle of the Alaskan wilderness, he could take her any time he wanted and no one would ever know.

They were married. Legally he had the right to take her into his bed…to claim her body.

To make her his wife in more than name only.

She glanced over at him, noting the thrust of his jaw, the sensual curve of his mouth. Those large hands that commanded the wheel. For an instant, she had a vivid image of how those hands would feel against her skin, cupping her breasts, sliding lower until she lost her mind.

If she hadn't already lost it.

"WHAT THE HELL?" Kiel slammed on the brakes a few hundred feet away from his cabin. There was no point to going any farther. There were enough autos, vans and trucks parked alongside the road, in the yard and in his driveway to fill a used car lot.

Lexi stared out the window. "I didn't think there were that many cars in the entire town."

"Neither did I," said Kiel. His anxiety level rose appreciably.

"What do you think's going on?"

"Beats me." He turned off the engine and reached for the door handle. "But I'm going to find out."

"Balloons!" Kelsey shrieked, pointing toward the house. "We're having a party!"

Lexi and Kiel locked glances.

"They wouldn't," she said.

"They would," said Kiel.

And they had.

Chapter Six

"They're here!" Agnes Lopez stood in the doorway and clapped her hands. "The newlyweds are here!"

Kiel didn't know whether to laugh or reach for a loaded weapon. All of PAX's brilliance and he'd forgotten one simple thing: he hadn't locked the front door. Thank God they hadn't been able to get into his lab. One wrong move and Alaska would be blasted back to the Stone Age.

"Smile," he said through gritted teeth as he helped Lexi and Kelsey from the Jeep.

Lexi rummaged through her purse. "I must have cried off all my eye makeup."

"You look fine."

"I can't look fine. My nose gets red when I cry."

"To hell with your nose," he said. "We have a houseful of strangers looking to toast the newlyweds. Try to act happy."

Kelsey didn't need any coaching. She broke free and bounded for the house. She was a bundle of enthusiasm, ready to embrace life with both hands, eager to discover what lay around the next corner. The way he used to be, back in the days when he believed in happy endings.

A long time ago.

Back when he believed love could make things right.

He reached for Lexi's hand. She looked up at him, a curious expression in her china-blue eyes. Her hand disappeared in his. A wave of emotion flooded through him, nearly bringing him to his knees. *You're beautiful,* he thought as they started toward the house. *I've never seen a woman as beautiful as you.*

He didn't know her. He didn't know anything about her. All he knew was the way she made him feel—vulnerable and a little less alone.

LEXI'S HEART thundered inside her chest. She'd held hands with a hundred men in her day. Maybe a thousand boys when she was a teenager. But that simple act had never made her feel as if she'd been drinking champagne.

More than anything, she wanted to pull her hand away from his, break the unnerving connection between them, but she knew she couldn't. This was part of the bargain and she'd sworn to do her best to maintain the illusion of a happy marriage. Six months from now it would all be over and this momentary discomfort would be forgotten. She'd be back in her real life where she belonged, with her inheritance tucked away in the bank doing whatever it was supposed to do to grow bigger and stronger.

She tossed her hair back from her face, and smiled up at her new husband.

"Ready?" he asked.

"Absolutely," she said.

SHE HAS GUTS, Kiel thought as they approached the throng waiting for them at the front door. She didn't know one damn person in the entire state but you'd never know that by looking at her. Shoulders back. Head high. A dazzling movie-star smile on her lovely face. If he didn't know better, he'd actually believe she was a blushing bride about to embark on a life of happiness and joy.

"Ain't you a pretty one!" Mr. Packer nodded his approval as he shook her hand. He winked broadly at Kiel. "And ain't you a sly dog for keepin' her a secret."

"Kiel's a very jealous husband," Lexi said, squeezing his forearm affectionately. "He wants to keep me all for himself."

He choked on his saliva.

"Are you all right?" she asked, all sweetness and solicitude.

"Fine," he managed to say after a moment.

Lexi turned back to the crowd. "I'm terrible with names," she said with all the natural elegance of someone born to the spotlight. "Please, everyone, don't be shy! Introduce yourselves."

They adored her instantly. In one hour she made friends with every one of the townspeople jammed into his log cabin. And she wasn't terrible with names. There must be a computer chip or two hidden away beneath that silky mane of blond hair because she seemed to find something unique about each individual she met, something that made him or her stand out above the crowd—and she remembered it.

He watched as she chatted with Agnes Lopez and Imelda Mulroney, two of the biggest gossips on the Nowhere grapevine. Agnes was blatantly checking out Lexi's blond hair, her blue eyes, the expensive clothes on her slender figure while Imelda conducted a more subtle survey of the same attributes.

And Alexa knew what they were about. He could tell by the way she made certain the two old biddies got a good look at the plain gold band PAX had had waiting for them at Judge Moreland's office. Agnes's eyes met Imelda's and their eyebrows lifted in perfect sync. *Sensible,* Agnes mouthed over Lexi's head. *Real people,* mouthed Imelda.

Laughing, he turned away. Lexi was about as sensible as a diamond-studded flea collar, but he no longer wondered what her value was to PAX. A potluck party in a log cabin in Alaska was about as alien to her as being happy was to him. But she did a hell of a lot better job at fooling people than he ever could. She laughed, she talked, she flirted with the old men and kept the younger ones at bay.

And it didn't take much effort to imagine her doing the same thing in some fancy drawing room in Paris or London or Rome. Or to imagine her gracing the arm of a powerful man, sharing his bed and stealing his secrets, all in the name of saving the world.

"Is something wrong?"

He looked down at Imelda Mulroney. "What makes you ask that?"

"The look on your face. You were about a thousand miles away."

"I guess I was." He glanced around. "Where's Kelsey?"

"Watchin' a video with one of my grandbabies."

He nodded. "What about Lexi?"

The expression on Imelda's face shifted. "Don't really know. Last I saw, she was shootin' the breeze with one of those trappers from over Pike's Leap way."

He scanned the room. "Where?"

Imelda's eyes held a twinkle. "Don't really remember. I think ol' Harry Blackburn's got himself a case on the little missus. Better stake your claim before he carts her off to his shack for the winter."

The last thing he had to do was stake his claim. Hell, there was no claim to be staked, except in the eyes of his neighbors. *This has to look like the real thing,* Ryder had said to him the other night when this ridiculous plan was first hatched. *The point of this marriage is to keep your neighbors at bay.*

Obviously no one at PAX had counted on those neighbors turning out to be more determined than General Patton during World War II. The whole thing amazed him. He was a virtual stranger. No one had even heard of Lexi until the day before she arrived. Yet the residents of Nowhere were treating them to a wedding celebration as if he and Lexi had lived there all their lives.

People were everywhere. Babies. Little kids. Parents of all ages. Trappers and loggers and women who'd made their living a long time ago keeping trappers and loggers warm through the endless Alaskan winters. He thanked whatever lucky stars he might have that all of his research papers and equipment were safely locked away in the bunker that served as his lab.

Tabletops were piled high with food, most of which he didn't recognize. Beer bits, something Imelda had called reindeer steaks, halibut cooked outside over a wood fire. They'd opened their hearts and their larders to throw this party and he found himself embarrassed to be the recipient under false pretenses.

He made his way through the noisy crowd in search of his temporary bride.

"We want pictures of the happy couple!" a burly man in a green flannel shirt called out, clapping Kiel on the back as he moved past.

"It's almost time to cut the weddin' cake," Connie Alfonsi reminded Kiel as he stood in the doorway to the kitchen. "You find that pretty little gal of yours and we'll get on with the festivities."

Festivities, he thought, glancing around the kitchen. What the hell was he doing having festivities? He wasn't here for festivities. He was here to find a way to keep the world from blowing itself up. Who would have figured his own solitary existence would be the first thing to explode?

She wasn't in the living room or the dining room or the kitchen. He damn well better not find her in the bedroom with one of these local Lotharios. They might be married in name only, but he'd gone through that kind of hell once in his life and he didn't intend to go through it again...not for PAX or anyone.

He was about to leave the kitchen and make the long march down the hallway toward the bedroom they were almost sharing when a movement beyond the window caught his eye. Lexi, minus her coat, stood near the door to his lab. Her arms were wrapped around her chest and even from this distance he could see she was shivering. What the hell was she doing out there? He'd told her his lab was off-limits. If PAX had any ideas about checking up on him, he'd be more than happy to tell them what they could do with their half-assed suspicions.

Loaded for bear, he flung open the back door and was about to roar his displeasure when he realized she wasn't alone. A short, stocky man with a shock of wild black hair had her engaged in animated conversation.

Still fuming, Kiel stalked across the snow-crusted yard to her side.

Her smile was radiant but he recognized the tension at the corners of her mouth.

He put his arm around her shoulders in a proprietary gesture. She snuggled close to his side.

He met the man's eyes. "I don't think we've met," he said with false cheer. "Kiel Brown."

The man offered his hand. Kiel shook it.

"Harry Blackburn. Heard you got some specimens of the great horned trout in that lab of yours. Thought I'd take a look."

"My lab is off-limits."

Lexi's smile grew wider. "Even to me," she said, dimpling. "Can you imagine that?"

"You're one of those environmental types," Blackburn said.

Kiel met the man's gaze straight-on. "That's right."

"One of those tree huggers."

"I've been called worse."

"Kiel is studying the migratory patterns of various local animals," Lexi said with a dazzling display of pearly white teeth. "I'll bet he knows just about every bird and bear within a hundred miles of here."

Thanks a lot, he thought.

Blackburn considered him thoughtfully. "So you know the name of every bird in these parts."

A pop quiz. Just what he needed. "I know the Latin names for three hundred and forty-two species of bird seen in Alaska and the Yukon Territory. Most of those names you've never heard of." If you're going to lie, lie big.

"I got a good eye for birds." Blackburn pointed toward a small brown clump of feathers sitting in a spruce tree nearby, chirping his little socks off. "What do you call that one?"

Tweetie-Pie, thought Kiel. "Ornithalius Marcus Aurelius."

Blackburn remained unimpressed. "Around here we call it a brown tree hatch."

"That's why I'm a scientist and you're not." He flexed his biceps noticeably and Blackburn beat a hasty retreat.

"I can't believe you did that," Lexi remarked when Blackburn was out of earshot. "What were you going to call the next bird he pointed out—Julius Caesar?''

''Either that or Circus Maximus.''

''Why didn't you just use their real names?''

Good question, Alexa Grace. ''More fun this way.''

''You're a wicked man,'' she said, turning her considerable charm in his direction. ''Mr. Blackburn didn't know what hit him.''

Kiel took a long look at the door to his lab. There were a few new scratches around the secondary lock that hadn't been there last night. ''What was the bozo doing when you found him?''

''Pushing at the door, looking around for a window he could peek through.''

''Exactly why I don't have windows.''

She considered him for a moment. ''I was wondering about that. How on earth can you stand not having windows?''

''Occupational hazard,'' he said, struggling to stay one step ahead of her. ''My lab is climate-and-light controlled for optimum working conditions.''

''Now I'm really confused,'' said Lexi. There was a lot more going on behind those china-blue eyes than she liked to let on. ''I thought environmentalists did their thing in the great outdoors, not cooped up in some stuffy concrete box.''

''Depends on the environmentalist.'' It occurred to him that he still had his arm around her shoulders. It also occurred to him that he liked it. A lot.

''Come on, you two!'' Agnes Lopez, hands on her ample hips, appeared in the back door. ''Everyone's ready for the cake-cutting ceremony except the bride and groom.''

''I guess that's us,'' said Lexi.

He nodded. ''Like it or not.''

She draped her arm about his waist. ''I can put up with it if you can.''

''Hell,'' he said. ''I got through six years at M.I.T. I can get through anything.''

WHAT ON EARTH was wrong with her? Ever since she'd arrived in Nowhere, she'd been acting like a sentimental idiot.

When she and Kiel walked into the living room and she saw all of those eager faces looking at them with such happiness, so much hope, she felt like the worst kind of fraud. Tears stung her eyes and she prayed their visitors would mistake them for tears of joy. These people believed in true love, in happily-ever-afters. A marriage of convenience would break their romantic hearts.

''Now both of you hold the knife,'' the woman named Agnes instructed Lexi and Kiel while Kelsey leaped about in excitement. ''We have to take some pictures.''

''Smile,'' she murmured to Kiel. ''You're supposed to be a happy bridegroom.''

''I'm doing the best I can,'' he murmured back.

It must be hard on you, she thought in a rare burst of understanding. They guided the knife through the layers of wedding cake. He'd been through all of this once before…and with a woman he loved. A woman

Anything less than a three-dimensional, technicolor kiss wasn't going to satisfy them.

Besides, there was the matter of male pride to consider. Something that had taken one hell of a beating when Helena left him for another man. Left him, left his daughter, left the life they'd shared, their dreams for the future.

He pulled Lexi close. She melted against him like warm silk. He wondered how many men she'd melted against just like that, all in the name of duty.

"Come on!" someone shouted. "We don't got all day."

She said nothing. Just looked up at him with the bluest eyes he'd ever seen.

"Hell," Kiel said gruffly. "Let's do it."

He heard the low rush of breath as he claimed her mouth. Her lips were soft, even softer than yesterday. Softer than a dream. The scent of lilacs filled his head as her arms slipped around his waist. He deepened the kiss. He couldn't help himself. She tasted of sugar and the sharp edge of danger. He'd forgotten how much he liked danger....

LEXI FELT as if she were standing at the edge of the world, ready to spin out into the blackness of space. *How ridiculous,* she thought as he deepened the kiss.

How perfectly wonderful...

She'd been kissed other times by other men. Experienced men. Men who knew their way around a woman. But not one of those kisses had stolen her breath. Not one of those kisses had made her feel that all things were possible, that the world was a magical place and she had only begun to discover its secrets.

His tongue slid across the place where her lips met.

Questing.

Demanding.

She forgot where she was. She forgot who she was. Her lips parted and she gave herself up to sensation.

The kiss they'd shared yesterday in front of MacDougal had been powerful, but it hadn't prepared her for this sensual onslaught. And he felt it, too. With their bodies melting together in an embrace, she could feel him growing hard against her and she felt a deeply female sense of both excitement and satisfaction.

Dimly she was aware of cheering, of the sounds of celebration, of a little girl's voice and the laughter of adults.

It didn't matter. Nothing mattered but that kiss...and her wish that it would never end.

Seconds or hours passed...she didn't know. Then suddenly, the world came rushing back at her in the form of a little girl tugging at her skirt.

"That's all!" said Kelsey sternly. "Enough kissing."

No, thought Lexi even as she laughed with the rest of the crowd. *Not enough...not nearly enough.*

Chapter Seven

They left behind homemade breads and home-brewed beer, enough cakes and cookies and stews to last the newlyweds until spring. And they left wedding gifts as well. Hand-crocheted doilies, brightly colored mittens, blankets and quilts and potpourris made to sweetly scent a lingerie drawer. Both she and Kiel studiously avoiding mentioning the shiny red box of condoms some thoughtful joker had provided.

Imelda Mulroney had taken it upon herself to turn down the covers on the king-size bed and sprinkle rose petals on the pillows.

"It's a custom in these parts," the woman said when Lexi caught her in the act. "We're not long on sentiment but we got a soft spot for newlyweds and babies."

Fertility, Imelda went on to explain. Fertility and happiness and long life.

Which just about covered the spectrum of human existence and eliminated Imelda as the donor of the condoms.

Kelsey, with a great deal of grumbling, was down for a nap. She'd been operating at full-speed since she woke up this morning, and when Kiel found her asleep over her slice of wedding cake, he and Lexi agreed a nap was a good idea.

Lexi wasn't so sure about that when she and Kiel found themselves alone in the quiet house.

They'd been alone last night but it hadn't felt anything like this. Last night there had been a certain energy between them, but that energy had been more the product of conflict rather than chemistry.

The kiss they'd shared over the wedding cake had changed everything.

Or had it?

She looked at Kiel. His dark hair fell across his forehead in shaggy disarray. The faintest hint of five o'clock shadow was visible along the strong curve of his jaw. The expression in his eyes gave away nothing.

He started to say something but caught himself.

A moment passed.

He glanced out the window toward the yard and his lab beyond. "I'd better get to work."

She nodded. "Fine. I guess I'll put all this food away." She gestured toward the mounds of leftovers piled high on the counters.

He pointed toward the telephone on the wall. "If there's an emergency, dial 88."

"Fine," she said again.

"You can handle dinner?"

"Thanks to the neighbors, I can handle dinner for the next six months."

A second later he was gone. She stood at the window and watched as he crunched his way across the thin layer of snow and ice that blanketed the yard. He paused in front of his lab, pressed some buttons, waited, pressed some more, then disappeared inside. The sound of the lab door closing behind him sounded like the dull thud of a bank vault being locked for the night.

Denali shimmered in the distance, snow-covered and bathed in the reddish-orange glow of sunset. Lexi's breath caught in her throat and a feeling of wonder washed over her. Man had yet to create anything more beautiful than the artless magic of nature. Was it any wonder people like Kiel were giving their time and expertise to preserve that beauty for future generations?

She frowned, retracing Kiel's progress across the backyard. He hadn't seemed to notice any of the beauty right under his nose. Or the eagle soaring overhead.

He was an environmentalist who seemed to relate to his environment about as well as Lexi related to housework. Wouldn't you think he'd at least have a window in his lab so he could take a look at the natural world he was so busy cataloging? His Marcus Aurelius remark to Harry Blackburn had been very amusing but she had the strangest feeling that if push had come to shove, Kiel wouldn't have been able to come up with anything more convincing.

Call me if there's a problem, Joanna had told Lexi as they said goodbye at JFK.

"There's a problem," Lexi said out loud as she watched darkness descend upon Denali. "Oh, Joanna, there are a lot of problems."

He was too handsome, too sexy, too masculine for her own good.

And he was too needy, even if he didn't realize it yet. Beneath that rock-hard exterior hid a softer heart than he'd probably ever admit to possessing. Had that soft heart been broken by the death of his wife or had his heart been broken before the final goodbye?

Not that it was any of her business.

Funny how saying the words "I do" could turn an otherwise intelligent woman into a simpering fool. And his kisses didn't help matters, either. This was supposed to be a business venture, pure and simple, but it hadn't taken long for Lexi to realize there wasn't anything either simple or pure about their situation.

"Time to get a grip, Alexa," she told herself sternly. She'd take care of Kelsey, she'd do her best to keep the house one step away from being declared a health hazard, but when it came to Kiel Brown, it was strictly hands off.

"YOU HAD A *WHAT?*" Ryder O'Neal's voice boomed through the secured phone line in Kiel's laboratory.

"A wedding party," Kiel said with an edge to his voice. "And it wasn't my idea."

"Whose idea was it—Lexi's?"

"Not hers, either." Although if she'd had time, Kiel was sure she would have sent out engraved invitations and a request for gifts. "The neighbors surprised us."

"What the hell are your neighbors doing surprising you with a party?"

Kiel's temper grew hotter. "It was your idea to let them know I was getting married, boss," he snapped. "It was their idea to throw a party."

"In the local beer hall maybe, but in *your* house? How did they get in?"

"Imelda Mulroney's son is a locksmith." Not that Imelda had needed him since Kiel had obligingly left the front door unlocked. But no way was he telling Ryder that.

"Jeez," O'Neal breathed. "Did you—"

"No," Kiel interjected. "Everything to do with the project is in the laboratory."

"I'm surprised Mulroney's son didn't give that a try, too."

Kiel thought of the scratches he'd seen around the strike plate but said nothing. He doubted that O'Neal would care to hear the story of Blackburn and that rara avis, the Marcus Aurelius. He listened impassively as O'Neal read him the riot act, stressing the importance and secrecy of his work, the vital nature of Kiel's place in the PAX machinery. When O'Neal stopped for breath, Kiel got around to the real reason for his call.

"This isn't going to work," he said. "She's not what I was looking for."

"Tough," said O'Neal in the same congenial tone of voice he'd used to dress him down. "She's what we were looking for."

"She can't even boil water," Kiel complained loudly.

"I never said we were sending Julia Child."

"Julia Child would be an improvement." At least

he wouldn't be having erotic dreams on an hourly basis.

"What else is wrong with your new bride?"

"She has an attitude."

"So do you."

"She's asking questions about my work. Just how much did you tell her?"

"Nothing," O'Neal said. "She thinks you're an environmentalist."

"The hell she does. I thought PAX operatives were more discreet. She welcomed the neighbors with open arms. I caught her inviting Imelda and Agnes and their cronies back for lunch. You'd better pray we get snowed in for the winter soon or we'll be having overnight guests."

An alarming silence from the other end.

"Are you there, O'Neal?"

"She's new," O'Neal said at last. "She's learning the ropes."

"I'm sitting on top of enough nuclear energy to blast us into the next century, and you send me an amateur." Great, he thought with grim satisfaction. Nothing like bitching about someone else to take the onus off your own shortcomings.

"We do what we have to do."

"Why'd you have to do it with me?"

"Have you read a newspaper lately, man?" O'Neal exploded. "The whole world's going to hell and you're complaining because we sent you the wrong wife." PAX had been hypersensitive since the bombing of the World Trade Center in New York.

Kiel started to list Lexi's shortcomings but O'Neal

talked over him, detailing the disasters unfolding in the Middle East and the Balkans.

"We're trying to keep a lid on things," O'Neal went on, "but the situation's getting hotter every hour." The nuclear underground was making its move, offering payment in gold for weapons that would give it deadly credibility on the world stage.

Kiel listened in silence. What the hell could he say? In the scheme of things, Alexa Grace Marsden wasn't even a blip on the screen. All he had to do was keep his hands to himself, his mind on his work and his fingers crossed that the crazies in this world wouldn't blow everyone to kingdom come before he had a chance to score a breakthrough.

The first was difficult.

The second was imperative.

And the third was asking for a miracle.

Just another average day in Nowhere.

KELSEY'S BATHTIME was much less eventful than it had been the night before. Now that Lexi knew what genital configuration to expect, she found that all she had to worry about was keeping herself from tumbling into the tub with the wriggling child.

"Hold still!" she said for the fifth—or was it sixth?—time. "Let me rinse your hair."

"I can do it," Kelsey said, her stubborn little chin thrust forward. "Daddy lets me do it."

"Well, I'm not your daddy and I think I should do it for you."

"You'll get soap in my eyes."

Lexi leaned back on her heels and looked at the

child in mock dismay. "I will not! I happen to be a first-class, world-champion shampoo rinser."

Kelsey giggled. "No, you're not."

"Oh yes, I am."

Kelsey shook her head and soap flew about the tiny bathroom.

"You look funny!" Kelsey said, giggling louder. "You have soap on your nose."

Lexi made a big production out of dispersing the offending bubble of shampoo. "I bet I can rinse all the shampoo out of your hair and your eyes won't sting a bit."

"Only Daddy can do that."

"I can do it, too."

"Will you read me a story afterward?"

The nanny's name was Sarah and she never had time for stories. "You know I leave at seven o'clock, Alexa," she'd said. "I can't stay late just to read to you."

The next nanny's name was Margaret. She lived in but she didn't believe in fairy tales. "No sense filling your mind with a lot of useless nonsense," she'd said when Lexi begged. "You're never too young to learn there are no happy endings...."

Lexi swallowed hard. Where on earth had that ridiculous lump in her throat come from, anyway? "Sure I will. But if we don't rinse your hair soon, you're going to turn into a waterlogged old prune."

"You're silly."

Lexi pushed her sleeves farther up her arms. "I've been called worse."

The shampoo was rinsed off in record time and

Lexi thanked the powers-that-be for the beloved toy poodle who'd shared her teenage years. Who would have imagined that washing mud off a dog's coat could help prepare you for motherhood?

"All done," she announced, lifting the little girl from the tub and bundling her in a big towel the way Kiel had done the previous night. She wrapped a smaller towel around Kelsey's head turban-fashion. "Now where are your pajamas?"

Kelsey pointed toward the hallway. "In the cupboard."

"Start drying off," Lexi instructed, "while I go get them."

The cupboard Kelsey referred to was a small linen closet midway between the master bedroom and the child's room. Lexi rummaged through haphazardly folded sheets and towels until she found a pair of ghastly looking pajamas with some horrid pizza-eating turtles painted on the jacket.

"These are terrible," she said, carrying them back into the bathroom. "Don't you have any nightgowns?"

Kelsey shook her head. "I got the Ninja Turtles for my birthday."

Lexi thought for a minute. "Would you like to sleep in a yellow gown?"

Kelsey's eyes widened. "Like Belle wore when she danced with the Beast?"

"Well, not exactly," Lexi said, "but almost as pretty."

"I can?" Kelsey asked. "Really?"

"You finish drying yourself off and I'll be back in a jiffy."

Two minutes later, Lexi returned with the jacket of her favorite pair of lemon-yellow silk pajamas. Nuns in a French convent had embroidered tiny white roses along the roll of the collar and at the points while a vine of morning glory curled along the lapels and graced the breast pocket.

"Oooh." The child's sigh filled the bathroom. "That's pretty."

"I know," said Lexi, thinking about those French nuns and all their hard work. "I must be crazy."

"I can really wear it tonight?"

It was Lexi's turn to sigh. "You can really wear it tonight." She slipped the child's tiny arms into the sleeves, buttoned up the front, then rolled the cuffs back three times until they just grazed Kelsey's wrists. The jacket itself reached her ankles. "Now we have to do something about that hair."

Kelsey, who was staring at her reflection in the foggy mirror, met Lexi's eyes. "Daddy makes two ponytails. He says that's what little girls always wear."

"Your daddy is a very fine man," Lexi said firmly. "And he's very smart, but he doesn't know anything when it comes to little girls."

"My daddy knows everything." Her small chin was set in the stubborn line Lexi was fast becoming familiar with. "He's the best daddy in the world."

"I know he is," Lexi said, "but not even the best daddy in the world can fix your hair the way I can."

"Hair ribbons are stupid," Kelsey said, making a face.

"How do you know?" Lexi asked smoothly. "Have you ever worn hair ribbons?"

She shook her head. "Aunt Edie wore hair ribbons to bed and they looked dumb."

"Okay, no hair ribbons. But I can still make you look as pretty as Belle."

"Really?" Kelsey didn't know whether to be dubious or thrilled.

"Really."

Alexa Grace Marsden might not know much about geography or physics but she defied anyone to tell her she didn't know hair.

She sat the little girl on the closed lid of the toilet seat and went to work.

"You have very pretty hair," she said as she gently eased the comb through the tangled waves. "Such a pretty shade of dark brown."

"My mommy had brown hair, too." Kelsey said it in a very matter-of-fact fashion.

Lexi took her cue from her. "Do you look like your mommy?"

Kelsey started to nod her head, then stopped so as not to disrupt Lexi's ministrations. "My aunt said I did, but Daddy never says anything at all."

Lexi continued easing the comb through the many tangles. Was he brokenhearted with grief and that's why he couldn't speak about his late wife? Why was it that she couldn't quite believe that to be the case?

Wishful thinking, a small voice mocked.

"Ouch!" Kelsey turned to look up at Lexi reproachfully. "That hurts."

"I'm sorry, honey." She kissed the top of the child's head, struck all at once by how tiny she was, by the fragrant sweetness of the damp waves, by the surprising twists of fate that had brought her to this place.

Remember, you're in it for the money, that same small voice reminded her. *Don't pretend you care for this child.*

"I do care," she said out loud, then stopped, her cheeks flaming with embarrassment. She cleared her throat as Kelsey continued to watch her with open curiosity. "I *do* care that you have the prettiest hairdo in all of Alaska!"

She set back to work with renewed enthusiasm, pouring her heart and soul into the project as if her very existence depended upon the outcome. She found a cloisonné comb in the drawer of Kelsey's nightstand. She even retrieved her blow dryer from one of her suitcases and finished off the little girl's bangs with a flourish.

"You're a vision of loveliness," she intoned as she stepped back to admire her handiwork. "Miss America!" Kelsey reached up to touch her hair, but Lexi grabbed her tiny hands and held them tight. "No, no! First you have to see how pretty you look."

With great ceremony she helped Kelsey to her feet, then led her to the mirror over the sink. It wasn't a perfectly lighted boudoir mirror but it would do in a pinch.

"Voilà, mademoiselle!" she said with a flourish. "I present the beautiful Miss Kelsey Brown!"

The child stared at her reflection for what seemed like the longest time. Lexi found herself shifting her weight from her left foot to her right as she awaited the verdict.

At last the little girl spoke. "Is that me?"

Lexi sighed with relief. "Of course that's you, honey."

"I'm pretty!" said Kelsey, trying to scramble up on the sink so she could get closer to the mirror. "How did you do that?"

"You always *were* pretty," Lexi said. "All it took was a little attention to detail."

Kelsey's eyes sparkled with pleasure. "I want to show Daddy how pretty I am."

Lexi hesitated. "Your daddy said we should only call him if it's an emergency."

"This *is* a 'mergency," said Kelsey. "I've never been pretty before."

That darned lump was back in Lexi's throat. *Daddy, look at me! Don't I look pretty in my new dress?* She couldn't have been any older than Kelsey, twirling before her father, being warmed by the look of pride and love on his face.

"Are you crying?" Kelsey asked.

"Just a little," said Lexi.

"Why?"

"I was thinking about my father."

"Do you miss him?"

She nodded, blinking quickly. "Very much."

"Where is he?"

''He's—'' She hesitated, then opted for honesty. ''My father's dead.''

Kelsey considered her words. ''My mommy is, too.''

''I know.'' Her voice broke on the last word. Good grief, this was turning into an emotional mine field.

''Sometimes I'm sad.''

''Me, too,'' said Lexi.

''Daddy said that my mommy loved me a lot.''

''I'm sure she did.''

Suddenly the child slid to the edge of the sink and wrapped her arms around Lexi's neck. ''I bet your daddy loved you too.''

''I know he did, sweetheart.'' *I want you to have a family,* he'd told her not long before he died. *I want you to know how it feels to love someone more than life itself.* Her father had felt Franklin was the man of Lexi's dreams and all Lexi needed was a push in the right direction. Little did Brandon Marsden realize his daughter would marry an utter stranger in order to collect her inheritance. *You meant well, Daddy, but look where I ended up.*

''I'll tell you what,'' she said to Kelsey. ''Maybe we should call your daddy after all and ask him to come in and see how pretty you look.''

The expression on the child's face was worth risking Kiel's wrath.

She took the child's hand and together they went into the kitchen to make the call.

Chapter Eight

"I'm going to kill her," Kiel muttered as he stormed across the icy ground toward the back door of the cabin. He'd been deeply engrossed in his work, certain he was about to unravel one of the knottier problems he'd been faced with since beginning the project, when the damn phone rang.

"It's not an emergency," Lexi had said first thing, "but you have to come over for a minute."

He'd complained loudly.

She overrode his objections.

And he decided that the pleasure he'd get from reading her the riot act face-to-face far outweighed the inconvenience.

"Rule number one," he roared as the kitchen door slammed shut behind him. "An emergency means life or death. If you—" He stopped. And stared. He blinked his eyes and stared again at the incredible sight before him. "Kelse?" It couldn't be.

The tiny vision in yellow silk beamed at him. "Don't I look pretty, Daddy?"

It was hard to see through the haze of unexpected tears. He bent down and laid a careful hand against her silky hair. "You're the most beautiful girl I've ever seen," he said, meaning it with all his heart.

He admired his daughter as she twirled about, exhibiting feminine wiles he'd never realized she possessed. She ducked her head to tug at the collar of her nightgown and he saw the cloisonné comb. He'd given that comb to Helena on their first anniversary. It was one of the things she hadn't bothered to take with her when she left. "Why don't you go brush your teeth, Kelse, and I'll come tuck you in when you're ready."

She floated off down the hall in a cloud of baby powder and Chanel No. 5, her tiny feet in their Mickey Mouse slippers making soft noises against the bare wood floor.

"You see why I had to call you," Lexi said, a big smile on her face. "She was so excited—"

"Don't call me again." The intensity of his words surprised him but there was no denying the way he felt. "You're here to give me the chance to work, not to call me inside over trifles."

"Trifles? You saw her. She was dancing on air with excitement. Your approval means the world to her."

"That might be," he said, gut twisting, "but when I'm working, I expect to be left alone."

The light in her eyes dimmed. "You're a bastard," she said in a flat tone of voice. "A total bastard."

He said nothing. There was nothing he could say. What had happened between himself and Helena was his business. Sharing it with a stranger wasn't his style.

"Don't you have anything to say?" Lexi demanded.

"No," he said calmly. "I don't think I do."

With that, he turned and went back to the lab.

LEXI STARED after him in disbelief. She wanted to run after him, grab him by his biceps and shake some sense into him, but she'd have a better chance trying to tame a grizzly bear. In truth she didn't care what he did with his life or how he spent his time, but the fact that he could turn away from a little girl who so obviously adored him made her see red.

"Louse," she said to the closed door. She looked around the room for something to throw against the wall but it occurred to her that she'd only have to clean up the mess herself. At least back home there had always been someone to cart away the consequences of her bad temper.

Kelsey's voice drifted toward the kitchen. "Daddy! I want a story!"

She cast one last dirty look in Kiel's general direction, then hurried back to tell Kelsey a bedtime story about a bad-tempered dragon who didn't know when he was well-off.

IT WAS the comb.

That damned cloisonné hair comb.

The night Helena left, he'd found the comb sitting atop her dresser along with her wedding ring, some old love letters, and the phone number of Kelsey's pediatrician. For weeks he'd walked around in a haze. The last few months of their marriage hadn't been good by any means, but when she told him it was over, that it had been over for a long time, that there was another man, he'd felt as if he'd been poleaxed. The only thing that had kept him going was the baby daughter who looked up at him with eyes so like her mother's that he didn't know whether to laugh or cry.

There was no way Lexi could have known any of this. He doubted that Joanna O'Neal would have supplied the information. It wasn't something you casually dropped into a conversation with a woman you barely knew...even if that woman happened to be your new wife. *By the way, in case you're wondering why I'm acting like such a fool, let me tell you a little something about the first Mrs. Brown. Take my wife...please. What was that? Oh yeah. Somebody already did....*

"Son of a bitch." He'd really lost it back there. He didn't believe in letting your emotions get the better of you, especially not when it came to the past. He saw that haircomb on Kelsey's nightstand every single day and he'd managed to keep the memories at bay. But seeing that comb holding back his daughter's hair, seeing her so grown-up in her silky yellow nightgown, that look of feminine awareness in her dark eyes—it was like seeing Helena again.

But the best of Helena. The girl inside the woman he'd fallen in love with, the woman he'd married, the woman he'd expected to grow old beside.

It wasn't going to happen again. You could surprise him once, but after that his defenses were back up, his armor in place. None of this was any of Lexi's business and he'd make sure it stayed that way.

THE DRAGON STORY led into one about a little mermaid and a handsome prince, and that was followed by "Cinderella." Lexi was quickly running out of fairy tales and was afraid she'd have to resort to relating Elizabeth Taylor's eight marriages when Kelsey drifted off to sleep just before the happily-ever-after ending.

And not a minute too soon.

She wandered over to the little bookshelf near the window. Four slabs of yellow pine rested on white lacquered brackets. Brightly colored volumes of *Winnie the Pooh* and *Charlotte's Web* and Disney's versions of *The Little Mermaid. Beauty and the Beast,* and *Sleeping Beauty* were neatly stacked side by side. They were all wonderful, but what she needed was a big fat volume of the Brothers Grimm, a refresher course in fairy tales.

She reached for a picture version of some Hans Christian Andersen favorites and her eye was caught by a piece of paper peeking out from between the shelf and the wall. Stretching, she managed to pluck it out. It was a photograph.

The night-light glowed softly from the outlet near the baseboard. Lexi crouched and held the photo up to the pale pink light. She exhaled on a long breath. The woman in the photo was lovely. Long dark hair piled artlessly on top of her head, held by a cloisonné comb. Lexi looked more closely at the photo. Yes. It was the same comb she had used to hold back Kelsey's hair. The woman looked straight at the camera, her full lips curved in a half smile, the smile of a woman who knew her power and how to use it. It was Kelsey twenty years from now...and yet it wasn't.

There was something cunning about the woman's smile, something sophisticated and knowing and sly. To her surprise, Lexi found herself recoiling.

"Ridiculous," she whispered, returning the photo to the bookshelf. That was Kelsey's mother. Kiel's first wife. What on earth was the matter with her, reading a thousand dark emotions into the photo of a beautiful woman who was no longer alive.

At least there was one thing she was sure about: she wasn't jealous.

Not for a minute.

KIEL GAVE UP the ghost before dawn.

He couldn't think, couldn't concentrate, couldn't get last night's scene out of his mind. He'd been a horse's ass to let something as stupid as a hair accessory blow him out of the water that way.

Lexi probably thought he was crazy. Hell, he wouldn't be at all surprised if she'd called Joanna the second he slammed the door behind him, and begged the woman for a reassignment. Something easy. Maybe a midnight raid on Saddam Hussein.

He couldn't blame her. Better a certified madman than a suspected one.

If things didn't improve and fast, it was going to be the longest winter of his life.

And more than likely, the most unproductive one.

"Okay," he said as he locked up the laboratory and started for the house. He'd give it one more try.

He'd shower, change into clean clothes, plug in the coffeemaker, then extend the olive branch.

He hung up his jacket on the peg near the door and was unbuttoning his shirt when he saw her. She was curled up at the far end of the couch. A bed pillow was tucked under her head and two afghans and a quilt were piled on top of her slender form.

Her second night on the sofa. This wasn't going to work. His weight bench was shoved in a corner of the room. Before Kelsey came to live with him, he'd made a habit of pumping iron as a means of cooling off after a marathon session in the lab.

The dying fire cast a dim, wavering light across her face. Her eyes were deeply shadowed. Between jet lag and their wedding, the wonder was she hadn't fallen asleep on her feet hours ago. Sleep had always seemed a waste of time to him. As a kid he'd trained himself to get by on a minimal amount of sleep. As an adult he'd had so much he wanted to accomplish that he begrudged every second lost to things as minor as exhaustion.

"Lexi." He placed a hand on her shoulder. "Why don't you go to bed."

She murmured something and pushed her face more deeply into the pillow.

He shook her gently. "You'll be more comfortable in the bedroom."

No response. Just the deep, regular sound of her breathing.

She couldn't stay on the couch. Once he started pumping iron, the clink of the weights would be bound to wake her up. He didn't much want to have her watching him work out. Besides, he had the feeling she needed more than four hours' sleep to maintain that cranky disposition.

Bending down, he gathered her, and her myriad blankets, into his arms. She seemed weightless, ephemeral, he mused as he made his way through the hall to his bedroom. She murmured something low in her throat and pressed her forehead against his throat. A muscle in his jaw worked convulsively in response. He tried to ignore the other responses his body was making.

The room was dark. He didn't turn on the light. If she woke up and found herself in his arms, she'd probably let out a howl of protest that would scare the daylights out of Kelsey, asleep in the next room. Besides, he didn't need to turn on the lights. The room was laid out like a monk's cell. A simple dresser near the window. A large bed against the wall. He could tell one from the other in the dark.

He laid her down. She protested softly, clinging to him an extra moment as he settled the covers over her. He pushed the pillow closer to her and after a moment she curled up against it like a kitten seeking warmth and comfort.

He wasn't sure what she was wearing under those covers and considered turning back the blanket to see but decided against it. In old movies the hero always had to help the heroine out of her wet/cold/inappropriate clothes and into the proper sleepwear, but he was of the opinion that if a person is tired enough, he or she could sleep in a straitjacket.

No, if he turned back the blanket to see what she

was wearing, there would be only one reason: to see her naked. Which she might be. She hadn't been expecting him to return to the house so early. And she was wrapped in enough covers to drape a grand piano.

He remembered that Kelsey was wearing one of Lexi's nightgowns or pajamas or something. It wasn't that farfetched an idea to think that there was nothing between him and her naked frame except a few blankets and his waning self-control.

He pushed a lock of pale blond hair off her cheek. It felt like raw silk beneath his fingertips. He already knew that it smelled like lilacs in the spring. And that her mouth was sweet as honey. And he somehow knew how she would sound when passion carried her to the edge…low and urgent and unbearably, painfully erotic.

She mumbled something and stretched languidly. He stepped away, feeling both guilty and intrigued. All things considered, he'd rather not want her. Sex would only complicate the already-tangled situation in which they found themselves.

There were only two important issues at stake: his daughter and his work. He and Alexa Grace Marsden and how they felt—or didn't feel about each other—didn't matter a damn in the scheme of things. If he had a choice, he'd rather not want her. If he had a choice, he'd rather she looked like the back end of a bus and had a face to match. But she didn't. She was tiny, delicately made, beautiful…even if her sharp tongue and imperious manner could use some work.

But hell, no one was perfect.

Definitely not Lexi.

He grinned ruefully. Not even him.

Temptation was everywhere in that room. It wouldn't take much to push him over the boundary that he'd set for himself. He'd given into temptation a time or two in his day, and for the most part he'd found reality came in a poor second to imagination.

Cold comfort, but it was the best he could do at four in the morning.

Turning, he left the room and went to pump a little iron.

LEXI WOKE UP to brilliant sunshine.

"Good grief," she said, sitting up in bed. If all that blasted sunshine was any indication, it must be high noon. Or pretty close to it. She had to get Kelsey up, make breakfast, do the—

Oh my God!

She was in bed. She hadn't started out the night in bed. She'd started out on the sofa.

And to make matters worse, it wasn't just any bed, it was *his.* The scent of soap and spice was everywhere, on her skin, in her hair, burned into her brain. She fell back against the mattress and covered her face with the pillow.

What on earth was going on? They'd had a wedding yesterday, but she was reasonably certain they hadn't enjoyed a wedding night. And a woman wasn't likely to forget her own wedding night, was she?

She swung her legs out of bed and stood up, gasping at the bite of the cold wood floor. She quickly noted that she was wearing the same lace panties and

T-shirt she'd donned before going to sleep. A quick prayer of thanks seemed to be in order.

Of course, the question still remained—how had she ended up in the bedroom. She wasn't a sleepwalker and she wasn't prone to playing musical beds. Besides, she would have sooner slept in the bathtub than in his bed. Husband or not, there was something too intimate about sharing a mattress...even if they were sharing it at different hours of the day.

There was only one way she would have ended up in his bed and that was if the Incredible Hunk himself had put her there.

His hands against her naked flesh. His hot glance searing her skin. His dirty rotten imagination going into overdrive and taking her with it.

Furious, she stormed from the bedroom, down the hall and into the kitchen.

He was sitting at the table eating a bowl of cereal. She could hear Kelsey singing along with Big Bird as she watched television in the living room.

"How dare you!" she stormed as he looked up at her. "If I'd wanted to sleep in your bed, I would have marched in there and done it. You had no right to move me."

"The hell I didn't." His spoon clattered back into the bowl. Droplets of milk splashed across the tabletop. "You were in my space. I moved you. Case closed."

"Case closed?" She smothered the urge to hit him over the head with the box of cornflakes. "You have a whole extra house to call your own. You don't have any right to steal the living room, too."

"It's my house."

"It's mine, too."

"The hell it is."

"The hell it isn't." She waved her left hand in front of his nose. "We're married, buster, in case you don't remember."

His expression was far from blissful. "You make it hard to forget."

"Go ahead," she said. "Insult me all you want. It doesn't change the facts."

"I was here before you," he said with annoying male logic. "I set up the rules."

"And that gives you the right to take over the living room?"

"Yup."

She stepped closer to him, wagging her finger mere inches from his face. "It doesn't give you the right to pick me up like I'm a sack of potatoes and move me wherever you want."

"I tried to wake you up. You wouldn't budge."

She treated him to her most disdainful look. "You couldn't have tried very hard. I happen to be a very light sleeper. The least little thing disturbs me."

She'd never heard anyone guffaw before. "Better tell it to someone who hasn't heard you snore."

"I do *not* snore."

"No? Then that was a damn good imitation of a freight train you were doing."

That was the last straw. She swung at him wildly but he was too fast for her. He grabbed her by the wrist, bent her arm behind her back, then pulled her down onto his lap. Hard.

"Let me go," she ordered, considering the wisdom of kicking him in the shins.

"So you can take another swing at me? Not on your life."

"If you'd treat me like a human being instead of a hood ornament, maybe I wouldn't want to take a swing at you."

The look on his face was priceless. "A hood ornament? Where did you get that idea from?"

"I—I don't really know, but it's the way you make me feel."

He started to laugh. A deep, full-bodied laugh that she could feel vibrating through his chest.

She struggled against him. "I'd die happy if you'd let me have one clear shot at you." Death would be a small price to pay for the pleasure of smashing him in the nose.

He laughed harder. Tears welled in his eyes.

"You're pushing it," she warned. "If you don't let me in on the joke, I'll—"

"A hood ornament," he managed to sputter, still laughing. "That's what I thought when I first saw you."

"You louse! What a rotten thing to tell me."

"It's okay if I think it as long as I don't tell you?"

She tossed her head. "Something like that. You don't see me telling you what I thought when I first saw you."

"Go ahead," he said, still holding her fast. "I'm tough. I can take it."

Good grief, Alexa Grace. Don't you know when to shut up? "Never mind," she said primly.

"Tell me."

She considered feigning a swoon but decided he'd never fall for it. Not after she'd threatened to punch him in the nose. "I was disappointed."

His eyebrows lifted. "In what way?"

"You weren't what I expected."

"Not tall enough?"

"You're tall enough." Any taller and they'd have to raise the ceilings for him.

"You don't like men with brains."

She barely restrained an unladylike snicker.

"I know what it is," he persisted. "You like blonds."

"Oh, for heaven's sake," she burst out. "If you must know, I thought you were too good-looking."

"You're kidding."

"No, I'm not kidding. I was expecting a more…cerebral type."

"I'm plenty cerebral," he said. "My IQ is one hundred and seventy-five and I have three degrees from MIT. I can't do the *New York Times* crossword puzzle in ink, but I can spell anti-disestablishmentarianism backward and with one lobe tied behind my back."

"You don't look cerebral."

"Neither do you," he said, "and you don't see me holding that against you."

"I'm *not* cerebral," she declared, as she struggled to climb off his lap. "I'm instinctual."

"Meaning what?"

"Meaning if you don't let me off your lap in the

next thirty seconds, you'll have fathered your last child."

"That's instinctual?"

"One hundred percent." When in doubt, go for the primal fears. It worked on Adam in the Garden and it worked on Kiel Brown in a cabin in Nowhere, Alaska. If that wasn't an example of instinct at work, she didn't know what was.

"A street fighter," he said, releasing her from his grasp. "At least now I know who I'm dealing with."

She stood up and moved just beyond his reach. A woman couldn't be too careful. "And who exactly am I dealing with?"

"Easy," he said, leaning back in his chair and reaching for his coffee. "A man who isn't looking for complications."

"Then we're in agreement. This is only a job."

"An assignment."

"A *temporary* assignment." She considered her next words carefully. "I doubt if we'll be together six months from now."

"I wouldn't go making plane reservations just yet, if I were you. There's no telling how long it'll take me to...monitor the migratory patterns."

"How long can it take?" she countered. "Once the winter's over and the birds quit migrating, your job's done."

"It's not that simple, Lexi."

"Of course it is." It was simpler than he knew. One day after their six months' anniversary, she'd be on her way out of Nowhere and back to life as it was meant to be lived. "All we have to do is keep out of each other's way."

He frowned. "It won't be easy in a place this small."

"You could sleep in your laboratory," she suggested helpfully.

"The hell I will. I'll sleep in my own bed."

"I could sleep in your laboratory."

"Over my dead body. No one goes in there but me."

"I don't see why you're so secretive about a whole lot of paperwork."

"You stick to your business, I'll stick to mine." He pushed back his chair and stood up. "And no more sleeping on the sofa. I use the living room around dawn to pump iron. You'll just get in my way."

He didn't look as if there was room for discussion in the matter. She shrugged. "It's yours. But on the slim chance you ever find me sleeping some place other than the bedroom, keep your hands off me."

"Agreed. Defined boundaries make cohabitation easier."

"Wow," she said dryly. "Is that your IQ speaking?"

"My common sense. If we give each other space, we'll keep out of trouble."

"Absolutely," she said. "And that will be much easier since we don't find each other attractive."

"Right," he said. "Definitely a lack of chemistry."

"And thank God for that," said Lexi. "Chemistry could make this arrangement very difficult."

He considered her for a long moment. She noticed his eyelashes were preternaturally long and curly, then pushed the thought from her mind. *No chemistry,* she reminded herself. *No chemistry.*

Chapter Nine

Living with a man, especially one like her new husband, brought with it a set of complications Lexi had never imagined. Even though he spent eighteen hours a day in his lab and slept for most of the remaining six, Lexi felt as if he were everywhere.

"No starch in the shirts," he said one morning as he passed through the kitchen en route to his lab.

"Don't tell me," Lexi said, looking up from her second cup of coffee. "Tell the laundry."

"That's a good one," Kiel said. "I like a sense of humor in a wife."

"If I weren't so tired, I'd throw something at you," she said around a yawn.

"Lexi!" Kelsey's high-pitched voice floated toward her from the front room. "It's time for 'Mr. Rogers'!"

Kiel was laughing as he closed the door behind him.

LEXI WOKE UP EARLY one morning toward the end of the second week. Squinting, she glanced at the clock on her nightstand. Five minutes after five. The last time she awoke this early was Christmas morning when she was six years old.

She closed her eyes. Nothing. She didn't feel even remotely sleepy.

She opened her eyes again. Like it or not, she was wide-awake.

"Make the best of it, Alexa Grace," she said, flinging back the covers. Take a shower, get dressed, then surprise Kiel with a homemade breakfast when he returned to the house after a night's work.

Clad in silk pajamas and bare feet, she gathered up her clothes, then hurried toward the bathroom. The door was ajar. A pool of light spilled into the darkened hallway. Kelsey, she thought as she pushed the door open the rest of the way, and another glass of water.

She stepped into the bathroom and was met by a burst of steam, followed by a roar of male outrage from behind the shower curtain.

"What the hell are you doing here?" her loving husband demanded.

"What are *you* doing here?" she retorted. "You should be working."

He glared at her from around the side of the curtain. "You should be sleeping."

"Excuse me for waking up early," she said edgily. "I thought I would take my shower, then make breakfast."

"*I'm* taking a shower."

"So I see."

"Yeah," he said. "And unless you want to see a hell of a lot more, you'd better get out of here."

"You don't have to be nasty about it," she said. "Believe me, you don't have anything I want to see." She paused, then summoned up a wicked grin. "At least nothing I can't see perfectly well through that shower curtain." She headed for the door. "They just don't make plastic the way they used to, do they?"

She thought she heard him laughing as she closed the door behind her.

SHE COULDN'T STOP thinking about the way he looked behind that transparent shower curtain. *Good grief,* she thought as she puttered about the kitchen. *The man has the market cornered on gorgeous.*

What on earth had Mother Nature been thinking when she parceled out physical attributes? Didn't anyone notice that Kiel Brown had received enough for five men? Just when Lexi had grown accustomed to his gorgeous face, she discovered that his body was bigger, better, more amazing than anything she'd imagined late at night, alone in the bed they almost shared.

Those powerful shoulders...that broad chest with the thick mat of dark hair...the narrow waist and—

She poured orange juice into Kelsey's oatmeal, put the milk away in the cupboard and didn't remember the bread toasting in the oven until smoke triggered the fire detector mounted on the far wall.

And wouldn't you just know he'd pick that day to join them for breakfast.

"Grown-ups are silly," Kelsey observed as Lexi placed a new bowl of oatmeal in front of her.

Kiel looked up from his coffee. "How come, Kelse?" he asked, eyes twinkling.

Kelsey told him about the juice and the milk and the toast.

"So I'm forgetful," Lexi said with a toss of her head. "So what?"

"Maybe you're distracted," Kiel said.

She glanced at him. "I can't imagine why."

"I can."

She lifted one eyebrow in what she hoped was a disdainful fashion.

He grinned. "Maybe you saw something that…unnerved you."

"Very unlikely. What I saw amounted to very little." It was his turn to look disgruntled and she laughed. "I may not be able to take it," she observed, "but I can certainly dish it out with the best of them."

"I'll remember to lock the bathroom door," he said.

"Do that," she said dryly. Faced with all of that male pulchritude for a second time, she wouldn't be held accountable for her actions.

WHILE SHE WAS in no danger of turning into the Happy Homemaker, Lexi settled into a routine with surprising ease. It wasn't much of a routine, all things considered, but Kelsey seemed content and the Incredible Hunk wasn't complaining.

In three short weeks she'd mastered the microwave, tamed the mysteries of the washer and dryer and learned to peacefully coexist exist with a four-year-old girl and her thirty-four-year-old father.

Not that she and Kiel saw much of each other. After the bathroom fiasco, both grew more careful about keeping their lives as separate as possible. While she never again caught him in the shower, he did catch her one afternoon in a very compromising position.

He'd been working hard on a particularly tricky permutation and decided he needed a break. He came back to the house, poured himself a cup of coffee, then proceeded to spill the whole damn thing on his shirt and pants. Muttering an oath, he headed for the bedroom to change.

And that's where he found her.

Her back was to him. Pale sunlight streamed in through the window, making her skin gleam like fine porcelain. And there was a lot of skin. Her gently curving hips were covered by a wisp of peach silk. A tiny, firm pinch of rounded derriere peeked out from the lacy edge of the leg openings. Her legs were surprisingly long for so small a woman. He grinned. They were damn fine legs at that. She was slipping into a wispy bra of the same peach color as her panties, and it occurred to him that, if he was lucky, he might get to see her breasts.

He wasn't lucky.

She fastened her bra, turned around, then blushed the most amazing shade of crimson.

"Don't worry," he said, his voice abnormally husky. "I didn't see anything."

"I'm not worried," she said, wrapping herself in the bedspread.

"You look worried."

"You're crazy."

"You have a great body."

"Thank you," she said with all the warmth of an Alaskan winter. "Now I can die happy."

"I would've said something but I didn't want to startle you."

"Right," she said. "And I was born yesterday."

"Look at it this way," he continued, thoroughly enjoying himself. "Now we can stop wondering what the other person looks like naked."

"Why, you—!"

She had great aim. If he hadn't ducked when he did, the slipper would have hit him right between the eyes.

ALTHOUGH SHE WOULDN'T admit it even to herself, the midday meal with Kiel and Kelsey had become the highlight of Lexi's day. She found herself planning the menu at night, fussing with her hair and makeup after breakfast, and hoping that a beautifully laid table could cover a multitude of culinary sins.

While he never said outright that he even noticed the trifolded napkins or the candles burning cheerfully in the middle of the kitchen table, he did seem to be making an effort to keep up his end of the conversation. He told outrageous stories about the dogs he'd owned as a little boy that had Kelsey laughing out loud but only made Lexi more curious.

"Pretty tame," she observed the first time he talked about Clyde the German shepherd with an overbite. "With your background, I figured you'd keep an ocelot or mountain goat as a pet."

He'd looked vaguely uncomfortable and sloughed

off her comment with a wisecrack that didn't do much to alleviate Lexi's initial assessment of his devotion to wildlife, both endangered and otherwise.

"You spend an awful lot of time indoors," she'd continued, curiosity pushing her forward. "I still don't understand how you can count migrating birds if you're not outside long enough to see any."

Alaska was a wildlife paradise. Even she, who wouldn't know a bald eagle from a nuthatch, found herself mesmerized by the sheer beauty of the land and its inhabitants.

"I mounted sensors in the area before you got here," he explained in a rush of scientific mumbo jumbo. "Now I have to take the raw data as it comes in and...."

Uh-huh, she thought, eyes glazing over as he talked on. *I'll believe it when I see you notice just one Alaskan sunset.*

"I THINK I have cabin fever," Lexi announced to Kelsey one afternoon following a particularly energetic game of Chutes and Ladders.

Kelsey, wearing her New York Yankees cap and one of Lexi's diamond bracelets, frowned up at her. "What's that?"

"A malady peculiar to adults with too much time on their hands."

Kelsey thought about it for a minute or two. "We could play Candyland."

"We played Candyland this morning," Lexi said, sounding not unlike a four-year-old herself.

"A movie," said Kelsey. Her blue eyes twinkled

with mischief. "My favorite movie in the whole world."

Good grief, thought Lexi. *Beauty and the Beast for the seventy-fifth time.* "Great, honey," she said with a sigh. "I'll make us some popcorn."

Ten minutes later, they were settled down on the sofa in the living room with a big bowl of popcorn between them. Kelsey had a cup of milk. Lexi had a diet cola.

"Now?" asked Kelsey, aiming the remote control at the television.

"Now," said Lexi. Did it matter that Gaston was beginning to look pretty cute to her? She grabbed a handful of popcorn, leaned back, then closed her eyes. First the legend about the spoiled prince and the curse placed upon him…then Belle as she drifted through the tiny French town…then the sound of Uzi submachine guns and—

She sat straight up. "Kelsey!" The screen was filled with firepower. "What on earth?"

"Rambo," said Kelsey, a beatific smile on her little face. "This is the best part."

Lexi grabbed for the remote control and stopped the tape. "I can't let you watch that—that trash! Your father would be furious."

Kelsey shook her head. "Daddy likes Rambo, too."

"I'll just bet he does," said Lexi, "but I can't believe he'd let you watch something this violent."

"He does," said Kelsey. "Lots and lots of times."

"Well, your daddy isn't here right now and I'm afraid I don't want you to watch it."

Kelsey's eyes narrowed. "You're mean."

Lexi nodded. "I suppose I must seem that way."

"My real mommy would let me watch Rambo."

Lexi didn't flinch. "Maybe she would."

"I'm not a baby. I can do what I want."

"You're not a baby," Lexi agreed, "but you are a child. And there are some movies that children shouldn't watch."

"But I've already seen it."

"Then you don't need to see it again." She got up and crossed the room. They kept videotapes in a big wickerbasket and Lexi rummaged around for something they could agree on. "*Old Yeller*!" A brand-new, unwatched copy. "This is a *wonderful* movie, Kelsey. You'll love it."

Kelsey looked suitably dubious, but Lexi was filled with enough enthusiasm for both of them.

In the lab Kiel let out a whoop of excitement. He wished Albert Einstein were around to give him a high-five.

This was what he'd been waiting for. The nuclear equivalent of the Rosetta stone. He'd been at it for twenty-seven hours straight, hot on the trail of a major breakthrough. It wasn't the answer to the problem, but it was the beginning of the answer and success was so close he could see it, even if he couldn't yet reach out and touch it.

He couldn't call O'Neal or anyone at PAX. That's not the way things were done. Information had to be passed through a series of encoding devices, processed, then transmitted in nontraceable batches. *Eureka* just wouldn't cut it.

He needed to talk to someone, to share the excitement if not the details. Kelsey might appreciate the fact that her old man was feeling pretty darned happy about something, but she wouldn't get the importance.

Hell, neither would Lexi but the thought of seeing her smile up at him with those big blue eyes of hers twinkling like starlight more than made up for that fact.

He powered down his equipment and locked the door behind him, remembering to activate the retinal I.D. device. People made mistakes when they were feeling cocky, and he was too close now to get sloppy.

Not that he had reason to believe anyone suspected him of being anything but the environmental research scientist he claimed to be. Once the wedding was over, he'd settled back into anonymity, which was exactly the way both he and PAX wanted it. Except for the occasional invitation to a potluck supper—which Lexi politely deflected—everything was back to normal.

If you could call being married in name only to a beautiful woman you barely knew normal.

He opened the back door and stepped into the kitchen. The smell of popcorn greeted him and his stomach rumbled in response. He couldn't remember when he'd last eaten. Yesterday morning? The day before? He didn't know. It was after four o'clock. Too late for lunch. Too early for dinner. Popcorn sounded perfect.

"Where is everybody?" he called out as he headed for the living room. "There'd better be some popcorn left or—"

He stopped in the doorway and stared.

Lexi was sobbing into a paper towel as if her heart would break. His little girl sat next to her, a wonderful look of concern on her face, as she patted Lexi on the shoulder and said, "It's only a movie."

He glanced at the television screen. "*Old Yeller*," he said with a shake of his head. "You were asking for trouble."

Lexi looked up at him. Her big blue eyes were drenched with tears. "Where were you when I needed you?" she managed to sputter through her sobs. "I'd forgotten how it ended."

"Daddy," said Kelsey. "Make her stop crying. It isn't real," she said to Lexi. "It's only a movie."

That didn't stop Lexi. In fact, it occurred to Kiel that she was actually enjoying the experience more than a little bit. He'd heard there were women who loved a "good cry" but he'd never actually met one.

"I don't think she wants to stop crying, Kelse," he said to his daughter as he rewound the tape.

"That's silly," said Kelsey. "Nobody *wants* to cry." She patted Lexi's hair with an awkwardly maternal gesture that put a big fat lump right in the middle of his throat.

"I don't know where my brains were," Lexi said, sniffling loudly and blotting her tearstained eyes with the edge of the paper toweling. "I always cry during Disney movies. Especially ones with dogs in them."

"Do you have a puppy?" Kelsey asked.

Lexi shook her head. "I had a puppy when I was a little girl. His name was Fred."

Kelsey looked up at Kiel. "I want a puppy, Daddy. Lexi had one when she was a little girl."

Thanks a lot, he mouthed over Kelsey's head.

Lexi grinned and shrugged her shoulders in a what-can-I-do? gesture.

"Fred?" he asked Lexi, grinning back at her.

"I was six years old and a major Flintstones fan. It seemed like a good idea at the time."

"Fred's not a bad name for a dog," he said.

She smoothed her pale blond hair off her face with a spare, elegant gesture that hinted at an upbringing a hell of a lot different than his own working-class background. "I'll have you know that Fred was short for Frederick, King of Dogs."

He turned his head away.

"Go ahead," she said airily. "Laugh if you like. Fred was an incredibly brilliant dog."

Kelsey tugged at the sleeve of his sweater. "You had a special dog when you were a little boy, Daddy, didn't you?"

Strange how those memories never left you. "Bingo," he said, ignoring Lexi's rippling laughter. "World's greatest mutt, second only to Clyde."

"Bingo?" Lexi asked, unable to contain herself. "You actually named your dog Bingo?" She rolled her eyes for his benefit as well as for Kelsey's. "Why not be original and call him Rover."

Even Kelsey, his traitorous daughter, found that one funny.

"Bingo was a canine genius," he said, not exaggerating a bit. "He could tell time."

"Daddy!" Kelsey's voice was choked with laughter. "Dogs can't tell time!"

"Bingo could," he insisted. "He'd be waiting at the front door for me every afternoon at three o'clock. He knew what time I got out of school and he was there waiting for me."

Kelsey sighed and pressed her head against his leg. "I want a dog, too."

"When we get back home you can have a dog," he said.

"But I want a dog now."

"Now isn't a good time to get a dog, Kelse."

Kelsey's chin trembled. He felt like the worst kind of rat. "Everyone has a dog except me."

Lexi, who had been listening quietly to their discussion, stood up and brushed popcorn from her lap. "You must be exhausted," she said to Kiel. "Kelsey and I will make supper while you play with your weights or whatever it is you do out here before you go to sleep."

"I'm not tired," he said.

"You should be. You've been working hellish hours." The look she gave him was frankly curious. "I'm still trying to figure out how you catalog wildlife when you never see any. When that moose strutted through the front yard last week, you didn't even act surprised."

"Not much surprises you when you live in Alaska."

"Maybe not," she said, "but I find it curious that a man who makes his living worrying about the natural world seems to have an aversion to it."

He met her eyes. "Let's go out for supper."

Her mouth dropped open. "What?"

"You heard me. Get your coat, get Kelsey's, and let's get the hell out of here."

He watched, mesmerized, as her eyes lit with pleasure. "Where will we go?"

"I don't know," he said. "Into town, maybe." An idea struck. "There's a roadhouse on the western edge that's supposed to have the best food around."

"That's not saying much," Lexi remarked dryly. "There's no competition."

Kelsey was bending G.I. Joe into painful contortions. "Hey, Kelse. What would you say about going for a ride?"

Kelsey's shriek of excitement was answer enough.

He grinned.

Lexi smiled.

It was going to be a great afternoon.

"STOP BEING RIDICULOUS," Lexi muttered as Kiel chatted with the old man at the filling station while the Jeep was being gassed up. "You're acting like a kid on her first date."

"What?" asked Kelsey from the back seat.

"Nothing, honey. I was talking to myself."

Kelsey giggled. "That's silly." She returned her attention to her coloring book.

Silly? No, it wasn't silly. It was insane, that's what it was. The three of them were going to some rinky-dink roadhouse for burgers and fries, and Lexi's foolish heart was doing backflips at the prospect. How utterly ridiculous could you get.

It's not like you're dating the man, she reminded herself as he climbed back into the car and she caught that tantalizing scent of soap and spice that she'd come to associate with him. *You're married to him!*

Which suddenly struck her as so outlandish that she started to laugh.

''Private joke?'' he asked.

She shook her head. ''Not really. It just occurred to me that we're married.''

He slanted a look in her direction. ''You just realized that?''

She met his glance. ''You must admit, this is not your conventional marriage.''

''No,'' he said, ''it's not.''

''They have a phrase for this in romance novels,'' she said. ''They call them marriages of convenience.''

He chuckled. ''Convenience isn't the first thing that springs to mind.''

''You have someone to take care of Kelsey,'' she observed. ''Surely that's convenient.''

He couldn't deny that. Unfortunately, neither could he deny the way he felt each time he climbed between the sheets and was enveloped with the scent of lilacs and of her skin.

He cleared his throat. ''One good thing,'' he said. ''At least we know this won't last forever. I—uh, I made some real progress the last couple of days. Things are moving along.''

''I don't know how you can be so sure,'' Lexi said. ''It's not even spring yet. You can't study migratory patterns until all the animals are finished migrating.''

She had a point. Too bad he couldn't tell her the truth. ''I've been here since May,'' he said as he veered the Jeep away from a ditch in the road.

''That long?''

''That long.''

They both fell silent, but the silence between them held a different quality.

IT CAN'T BE over this soon, Lexi thought. Six months. She'd been promised the six months she needed to claim her inheritance. That had been part of the bargain. *So why is it you feel sad, Alexa Grace, and not angry?* She should be furious that her fortune might slip through her hands. She should be looking for the nearest available telephone so she could call Joanna and read her the riot act.

Instead, she found herself thinking about Kelsey, her soft dark brown hair, her laughter...her father.

That's not possible, she thought, casting a quick glance in Kiel's direction. Oh, they'd reached an accommodation between them but nothing more. Except for sharing a midday meal, they rarely even saw each other. But that darn meal had become the best part of her day.

Kelsey obviously adored her father and there was no doubt that Kiel was equally crazy about his daughter. Did he see his late wife every time he looked at her? Lexi found herself wondering about that more often than she should. Her father had grieved for her mother until the day he died. No one had ever been able to take the place of Brandon Marsden's beloved wife.

Was it the same for Kiel? Did he think of Helena every day? Would he ever love anyone the way he'd loved Kelsey's mother?

How would it feel to love someone enough to pledge your life to her, to have a child together, then to see all of your dreams shattered by a tragic accident?

She wondered if broken hearts ever mended…and she wondered if it was any of her business whether or not they did.

Don't be a fool, she chided herself. *Remember this marriage is an illusion, not a reality.* And a reality of her own making. She'd gone into this with her eyes open and her priorities straight and if this marriage of convenience turned out to be more complicated than she'd expected, that was nobody's problem but her own.

There was something incredibly intimate about sharing a bed even if they never found themselves in that bed at the same time. She wondered if he thought about her when he climbed between the sheets. Did the scent of her soap linger? Did he even notice? Suddenly it seemed terribly important to know these things before it was too late and they went their separate ways.

WAS SHE CRYING?

He whipped the Jeep into the lot adjacent to Ranaghan's Road House. He set the parking brake and shot a sharp look in her direction.

Her eyes were wet.

With tears?

Get real, Brown. Why the hell would she be crying over you? Maybe she had a cold. Winter was in the air and she wasn't used to the bitter iciness of that season in Alaska. Neither was he, for that matter, but she was so small, so delicate, that he had trouble imagining her bundled up in a parka and battling her way to the woodpile.

Like you're going to ask her to cart firewood inside, that same annoying voice mocked him. He knew damn well he'd make sure there were plenty of logs stacked near the hearth.

Some marriage of convenience, Mr. Wizard. Why don't you just tell her to put her feet up and eat bonbons while you do all the work?

"Shut up," he muttered as he climbed out of the Jeep and went around to help Lexi and his daughter out. Kelsey obviously adored her. Anyone who could keep a four-year-old child happy, healthy and occupied twenty-four hours a day deserved his respect and admiration.

There's more, Superman. Why don't you admit it's true?

He swung open the door to the car and offered Lexi his hand. She met his eyes and smiled. His heart did a 360.

Told you so, said the little voice. *You're in trouble.*

RANAGHAN'S ROAD HOUSE looked like a set from an old John Wayne movie, one of those rough-and-tumble, good-natured, boys-will-be-boys movies that made Technicolor the success that it was. Lots of lumber, lots of laughter, lots of people.

Whatever hold on reality Lexi still possessed vanished the moment she stepped inside. The walls were covered with animal heads—moose, deer, assorted furry creatures—and dead fish mounted on polished wooden plaques beside signs that read, You Should Have Seen The One That Got Away.

Country music blared from the jukebox at the far end of the bar. Garth Brooks or Randy Travis or Gene Autry—Lexi couldn't tell the difference. A group of men in plaid flannel shirts crowded the bar while two middle-aged women sat at a table near the window and chatted amiably as they worked on their knitting. A knot of little kids laughed together at another table as they played a game of Chutes and Ladders. It took Kelsey all of ten seconds to join them.

"For heaven's sake," Lexi said as she watched the children welcome Kelsey into their group. "Those are the Mulroney grandkids."

The words were no sooner out of her mouth when Imelda and her husband bore down on them, filled with greetings and good cheer.

"Fancy meetin' you here," said Imelda, pulling Lexi to her bosom in an embrace. "Figured you'd be holed up in your house 'til spring."

"Cabin fever," said Lexi, wishing the woman had taken a lighter touch with her cologne. She looked over at Kiel who didn't seem too thrilled to bump into their neighbors. ''Kiel decided to take the afternoon off and take us out for lunch.''

Imelda released Lexi, then enveloped Kiel in a bear hug. ''Aren't you the most wonderful hubby in the world!'' She raised her voice to a stunning decibel level. ''Everyone, we have us some newlyweds!''

The men at the bar muttered something that sounded suspiciously like sympathy. The knitting women oohed and aahed their approval. Someone else called out, ''A toast to the newlyweds!'' and ordered the bartender to get out the Macnish and some glasses.

''What's Macnish?'' Lexi whispered to Kiel.

''Sounds like some kind of scotch,'' he whispered back.

''Best scotch in the known universe,'' said Imelda's husband who'd overheard them. ''But you need yourself an iron-clad stomach.''

Lexi opted for ginger ale while Kiel contented himself with a local beer. They listened while a seventy-something waitress read the specials off a chalkboard on the wall. Salisbury steak. Meat-loaf sandwiches. Cheeseburger.

''They're all hamburger,'' Lexi observed with a shake of her head.

They placed their own orders and asked for a plain hamburger and milk for Kelsey. The waitress bustled away, leaving the newlyweds alone together at their table.

''Imelda's watching us,'' Kiel said, draining his mug of beer.

''She has a soft spot for newlyweds,'' Lexi said.

"She wouldn't much like the truth, would she?"

"No," said Lexi, "I don't imagine she would."

"Daddy!" Kelsey popped up at their table. "Can I have a quarter for the games?"

"Your burger'll be here in a few minutes, Kelse. Why don't you wait?"

Lexi reached into her pocket and dug out a quarter. "Here, sweetie," she said, handing the coin to the little girl. "The first one's on me. Just make sure you're back here for your lunch."

Kelsey skipped away to rejoin the Mulroney grandkids. It was one of those easy, family kind of moments that happened a million times a day all across the country. One parent says no, one parent says yes, and the yes parent wins. Only thing was, it had never happened before with Kiel and Lexi. She hadn't given it a split second's worth of thought. Giving Kelsey the quarter had seemed as natural as breathing.

"I'm sorry if I stepped on your toes," she said, gesturing toward Kelsey who was playing at an old Ms. Pac-Man machine.

"No problem," he said.

"I didn't mean to override you."

"Don't worry about it."

"I apologize if I—"

He reached across the table and took her hand. "Enough," he said, his voice gruff. "You gave her a quarter, not a submachine gun. It's okay."

She couldn't help it. Her gaze dropped to their hands resting atop the table. His gaze followed hers. He didn't say anything and neither did she. They just sat there, looking at each other and holding hands while either Whitney Houston, Reba McIntyre or Dolly Parton sang loudly in the background.

He's doing this for Imelda's benefit, Lexi told herself. *So we look like real newlyweds.*

She's good, thought Kiel as he held her hand. *You'd think she really was a blushing bride.*

"Heads up," said the waitress. "Food's here."

He released her hand. Reluctantly.

She pulled her hand away. Regretfully.

"Kelse!" Kiel called. "Your burger's ready."

The waitress asked Kiel if he wanted another beer. She brought Lexi a second ginger ale. Kelsey took her seat at the table, her big blue eyes dancing with excitement.

"Daddy," Kelsey said, "can I have Nintendo at home?"

Kiel looked at his daughter and groaned out loud. Lexi couldn't help it. She threw back her head and she laughed.

Their moment ended.

But not the awareness that things between them were changing and there could be no turning back.

Chapter Ten

Lexi was laughing at one of the bartender's many stories about the time he tackled the Iditarod race when she saw a familiar face walk through the door. "MacDougal!" she said, pointing toward the burly pilot. "What on earth is he doing here?"

Kiel swiveled around in his chair to take a look. "Delivering another bride?" he asked dryly.

She swatted him with her paper napkin. "Very funny."

Imelda Mulroney didn't miss a trick. "Aren't you two the sweetest things ever?" she said in a syrupy tone of voice. "There's nothing in the world like young love."

"I'm almost twenty-five," Lexi said. "That's not all that young." In three days she'd reach the quarter-century mark and be of legal age to inherit her father's fortune. Provided, of course, that she remained married.

"Greetings," said MacDougal, as he approached their table. He was carrying a bottle of beer. "How's married life treatin' you folks?"

"Fine," said Lexi in a stiffly formal tone of voice.

"Did you rob any unsuspecting tourists of their hard-earned money today?" That four-hundred-and-fifty-dollar tab still rankled.

"Feisty as a polecat," MacDougal observed. He turned to Kiel. "Surprised you look so chipper, all things considered. She's the mouthiest woman I've ever met."

"Highway robbery is highway robbery," Lexi declared. "If you're going to overcharge your customers, the least you should do is take American Express."

"Angus is expensive," Imelda observed, "but he's the best bush pilot in the state. No one copes with overflow better than our Mr. MacDougal."

Overflow? Both Kiel and Lexi looked blank. Imelda explained that overflow was a "refreeze" situation that could trap a downed plane before a pilot had a chance to restart the engine.

"That's why we strap snowshoes under the wings," MacDougal said as he took a long sip of beer. "Never know what you're goin' to need or why."

"Aren't you just the world's oldest Boy Scout," Lexi muttered, trying to ignore Kiel's warning look.

"And how are those adorable grandbabies of yours?" Imelda asked.

"Fine and dandy. Got some new pictures you might like to see."

"Cute," said Lexi when it was her turn to admire the photos. *But not half as cute as Kelsey.*

"Cut him some slack," Kiel said quietly. "The guy's in business to make a buck."

"That's not what you said when I arrived."

"I wasn't expecting to foot the bill."

"Well, neither was I. I thought Ryder or Joanna would—"

MacDougal startled her by reaching for her hand. She hadn't realized the pilot had moved directly behind them. "That's Patsy Cline on the jukebox. How about a dance with the bride?"

Imelda clapped her hands with glee before Lexi had the chance to speak. "Dancin'! That's what we were missin' at your weddin' party. Our bride and groom have to dance!" She leaped to her feet. "Crank up the volume, Riggins!" she called to the bartender. "We're goin' to have us some fun."

"Not what MacDougal had in mind," Kiel observed as she stepped into his embrace. "He wanted to dance with you."

"Not what we had in mind, either," she said as his hand came to rest at the small of her back.

"Could be worse."

She smiled as they began to sway to the music. "A few weeks ago, you wouldn't have said that."

He looked down at her. "A few weeks ago, you wouldn't have danced with me."

"It's not as if I have a choice," she said primly. "We have to keep up appearances after all."

"Let's give 'em something to talk about."

"Kiel, I—"

He bent her back over his arm, low, lower, then lower still until she was laughing with surprise and pleasure. He brought her back up with one fluid movement, then swept her into a series of turns that had everyone stomping and whistling their approval.

"Music's over," MacDougal called out to the amusement of all. "Time to sit down, folks."

"They're in love," said Imelda Mulroney. "Ain't it romantic?"

"IMELDA MULRONEY TALKS a lot," Kiel remarked as they drove away from the roadhouse three hours later.

Lexi fastened her seat belt and chuckled. "She means well."

"How many times did she ask if Kelsey was going to have a baby brother or sister this spring?"

"I stopped counting at seven."

"You did a good job," he said, shooting her a look in the darkened car.

"So did you."

"I think they really believed we're newlyweds."

"We *are* newlyweds," she said with a soft laugh. "Just not for the reasons they think."

"What's that about a birthday party tomorrow?"

Lexi smiled. "Kelsey's so excited. Imelda's grandson is having a party and she's invited."

"I don't know about that—"

Lexi rummaged in her pocket for a piece of paper that contained a map. "All I'd have to do is drive straight down the road right into town. It shouldn't be hard to find."

They fell quiet for a few miles. Kelsey slept peacefully in the back seat. There was something hypnotic about the dark ribbon of road unfolding before the Jeep's headlights, washed silver by the glow of the moon that rode high in the sky. He still wasn't accustomed to the sharp clarity of an Alaskan night. A tree three hundred yards down the road was as clear to him as one that was close enough to touch, wreaking havoc with perspective and judgment. And that still didn't take into account the sheer, mind-blowing beauty of the northern lights, that shower of crystal in the obsidian sky.

A man couldn't trust his own senses in this strange and beautiful land, not until he'd grown accustomed to the wonder of it all.

Next to him, Lexi rolled down her window and looked out.

"...so amazing...," he heard her whisper.

Her pale blond hair shimmered in the moonlight. There was a look of such enchantment on her beautiful face, such wonder, that he found himself filled with a sense of hope he'd thought was gone forever from his life.

You're amazing, he thought, gripping the wheel more tightly. He didn't know anything about her except the way she made him feel and suddenly that seemed more than enough.

"Look," he said, braking to a stop. "Over there!" He pointed toward a heavily wooded area to the left.

"I don't see anything."

"About thirty degrees left of the fender."

She made a face and unbuckled her seat belt. "Sometimes you talk like a physicist." Her grin softened her words. "English, please."

He cupped her chin with his hand and turned her head in the right direction. "There."

Her slow intake of breath made him smile. "Ohh..."

The wolf watched them from the side of the road, eyes glittering and wary. He was a magnificent animal, broad across the shoulders, heavily muscled, a fierce intelligence evident in the proud lift of his head as he assessed them.

A moment later the wolf was gone, vanished back into the endless forest.

They drove the rest of the way in silence. But this silence was different from the silences they'd encountered in the past. There was nothing confrontational about it, nothing antagonistic. This silence was charged with something much more dangerous: an awareness of each other that deepened with every mile.

By the time he pulled into the rutted driveway next to the house, Lexi was finding it difficult to breathe. Anticipation was building inside her chest, a sense of inevitability she couldn't define. She'd never felt this way before. Each movement she made was fraught with meaning. Every breath she struggled to draw was filled with possibilities.

Ridiculous, she thought as she followed Kiel, with a sleeping Kelsey in his arms, into the house. All of this emphasis on being newlyweds was having an effect on her. And why not? Actors and actresses were always confusing theater with reality and that was exactly what was happening with her and Kiel.

She and Kiel were the leads in a very personal drama, one that she had to see through to the final curtain. Before tonight, she had been focused on the outcome, her inheritance. She'd never given any thought to emotional complications, mostly because she'd never believed there could be any.

Kiel switched on the light in the front room. Kelsey was sound-asleep in his arms, her head resting against his broad chest, her tiny arms wrapped around his neck. She looked so tiny, so vulnerable, so sweetly secure in her father's arms, that Lexi blinked back tears.

"I'm going to put her down for the night," he said.

"I think we can skip a bath tonight, don't you?"

He nodded. "She's had a big day."

"A great day," Lexi amended. "She was so happy that you spent the afternoon with her." Watching Kiel and his daughter play the video games at Ranaghan's Road House had brought back so many happy memories of her own time with her late father. "Life is so short," she said, embarrassed by the quaver in her voice. "Enjoy her while you can."

Their eyes met. There was an expression in his that she had never seen there before. Turning away, she headed for the kitchen to make a pot of coffee.

THE HOUSE SEEMED different somehow. Kiel couldn't quantify the difference but that didn't mean it wasn't real. The way the wind whistled past the house, the creaking sounds the floorboards made as he walked through the hall, the smells of woodsmoke and lilacs. It was all familiar, all strange, all miraculous.

He felt as if everything he saw and touched and heard was brand-new, as if he'd been walking through the past few years with his senses shut down to everything but the bare necessities of survival. Only Kelsey had been able to get beyond the boundaries he'd erected after Helena had left them for another life. *Another man.*

"Dangerous stuff," he muttered as he walked down the hallway toward the kitchen. That's how a man got into trouble, believing in what he knew wasn't true or real or lasting.

Like his marriage to Alexa Grace Marsden.

Like the way she made him feel.

Hopeful.

Hungry.

Too reckless for his own damn good.

Something had happened between them in the roadhouse. An awareness of a deeper need that had nothing to do with the business arrangement they called a marriage. Sexual chemistry played a part in it, but not even the powerful lure of sex could explain the tightness in his chest or the aching loneliness inside his soul. He only knew that when he was with Lexi, he felt alive in a way he'd believed lost to him forever.

There was only one thing to do: he had to put a stop to it and the sooner the better.

Like right now.

IT WAS a simple chore, making coffee. An enjoyable chore. In a pinch, even Kelsey could make coffee.

Tonight, however, Lexi was at a loss. She spilled water all over the floor. She scattered ground coffee beans across the countertop. Three filters, mangled beyond recognition, were sticking out of the trash can under the sink. She was working on a fourth, trying to settle it down in the basket, when she grew aware of Kiel standing behind her.

''Problem?'' he asked, his voice a long, slow, lazy rumble.

She shook her head, trying to blink away the idiotic tears welling in her eyes. ''Only if you consider terminal clumsiness a problem.''

The sound of his boots against the tile floor seemed to echo in the quiet kitchen as he approached.

''Let me do it.''

He was next to her, so close that she caught his scent of soap and spice and the sharp tang of anticipation.

''I'm all thumbs,'' she said, not moving away as he reached across her body for the box of filters. ''I don't know what's wrong.''

His hands were large, beautifully formed. Strong hands. She felt dizzy, as if the world she knew were spinning out of control and there wasn't a thing she could do to stop it. He opened the filter, placed it in the pot, measured out the ground coffee beans. Simple gestures but she watched them, fascinated.

He pressed the start button on the machine, then looked at her long and hard. ''So why are you crying?'' he asked.

Lying was the simplest answer to a question more complicated than she cared to acknowledge. It occurred to her that she could lie to him...she *should* lie to him. They meant nothing to each other. Honesty had nothing to do with the bargain they'd struck.

But she made a mistake. She looked into his eyes,

beyond his beauty, and something deep inside her heart began to thaw.

"My father," she said simply. "I still miss him."

Her words startled him. For a moment he wondered if this was part of the PAX-created scenario they were living, but there was no mistaking the bone-deep loneliness behind her words.

"How long?" he asked.

"Almost three years." She brushed a hand across her eyes and he noted the shadows beneath them. "When I saw you with Kelsey, I—" She shrugged her shoulders and he struggled with the urge to pull her into his arms and hold her close.

"Daddy's girl?" he asked, his tone softening the words.

She nodded. "Unashamedly so. He spoiled me rotten and loved doing it."

"Is that when you—" He caught himself. He'd been about to ask if that was when she'd hooked up with PAX. From the beginning, she'd seemed an unlikely candidate, but he knew firsthand the places where loneliness could take you. They were on dangerous enough ground as it was. One step further and he might compromise everything he'd worked so hard to achieve. "Forget I said anything."

She smiled briefly. "I could not ask you the same question."

"Doesn't much matter, does it?"

"Not very," she agreed. "We're both here."

"Yeah," he said. "We're both here."

He took a step toward her...she took a step toward him. For the first time, they found themselves in each other's arms for no one's benefit but their own. No audience. Nothing to prove. Nothing to be gained from the embrace except the knowledge that they weren't alone, that the world wasn't a dark and cold place, that if only for this moment in time, in this place, life was sweet and good.

This time she opened her mouth for him. Her lips parted. His tongue found hers, drawing her quickly into battle. She tasted the way he'd dreamed she would, sweet and hot, and her taste made him hunger for more.

She melted against him shamelessly. A warning went off somewhere deep in her mind. *You're playing with fire, Alexa Grace....*

Yes, she thought, as his hands slid up her rib cage and to her breasts. She was playing with fire and she knew it and, more than anything, she wanted to burn.

He broke the kiss, drawing his lips down the column of her throat. "What do you want?" he asked, his voice a low growl. "Tell me and it's yours."

How could she tell him when her mind was spiraling out of her body, floating freely into space. "I don't know—" Her voice caught on the lie. "Everything," she said after a moment. "I want everything."

It was all that he needed to hear. Grabbing her by the waist, he lifted her off the ground, then held her against his body, his powerful hands cupping her bottom.

"Wrap your legs around me, Lexi."

She heard his voice through a fog of desire so intense, she feared she would die of it. She did as he ordered, instinct, if not experience, guiding her. He leaned back against the counter and she felt the heat of his body against the sensitive flesh of her inner thighs. For weeks she'd been fantasizing about the way his body would feel against hers, but her dreams had fallen far short of reality. All of her dreams had. It was more than touch. It was taste and sound and smell and the deep blue of his eyes as he watched her watching him.

She trembled against him, making him feel all-powerful and oddly protective at the same time. What he wanted was to lay her down on the scarred maple table, rip her panties off with his teeth, then bury himself so deep inside her that when she came, he'd feel her climax rippling around him.

What he did was stroke her, move against her, kiss her in a way that left no doubt that he wanted more.

Much more.

IT WASN'T enough for her.

Not the deep wet kisses that stole her breath.

Not the powerful feel of his hands against her hips.

Not the fine and painful tension that coiled more tightly inside her body with each second, each moment, that passed.

She wanted...something. Everything. She wanted him, this stranger who was her husband. She wanted him recklessly, passionately, now.

She arched against him, aching for the sense of completion that eluded her. ''Not here,'' she whispered. ''Kelsey might—''

His kiss stopped her words. Before the kiss ended they were in the bedroom with the door shut behind them and that wide and welcoming bed they'd shared but never shared at all waiting for them.

They fell together to the mattress, limbs tangled, hearts thundering in anticipation. They struggled with their clothes, battling zippers and buttons and snaps, everything that delayed the wondrous shock of skin against skin.

There were no words, no whispered endearments, nothing but the blistering, primal heat that carried them closer and closer to the heart of the sun.

The sight of him, naked and erect, both thrilled and terrified her.

The sight of her, thighs parted, almost brought him to the brink.

He cupped her mound with his hand, feeling her heat against his skin, the slick wetness of her excitement.

Her back arched as she pressed against him, urging him on. She stroked his back with eager hands, found his nipples with her palms, then trailed down lower and lower until she encircled him. He was all heat, all throbbing life.

"Now," she whispered.

"Not yet." He got up and looked in the top drawer of the nightstand for a condom. "Great wedding present after all." He was back beside her a moment later.

The last of her doubts vanished.

He spread her thighs and poised himself between them.

She began to tremble with need. "I—"

"Shh."

He reached down and stroked her with his hand.

"You're ready."

"I know," she said on a moan.

He pressed against her. She opened. He moved slowly into the tight warmth of her body. It couldn't be…was she—

"You're a virgin."

She met his eyes. "You sound surprised."

"I am. You're a beautiful woman. I thought…" It didn't matter what he'd thought.

"I know what I'm doing." Her voice was soft but strong. "I want you to be the first man I make love with."

The words acted upon him like an aphrodisiac. Only the urgent desire to make her first time as pleasurable as she deserved it to be kept him from climaxing right then and there.

But there was so much he wanted to show her, the beautiful simplicity, the dark ecstasy that a man and woman could find in each other's arms.

He pressed harder, harder still, and the barrier was gone. She bit back a cry and he covered her face with kisses both hot and tender and filled with promise.

"Ride with me, Alexa Grace," he murmured into her ear. "Let me take you the rest of the way."

Chapter Eleven

When it was over, when she could think again, Lexi said, "I had no idea. I mean I've read about it and I've wondered about it, but I never ever thought—"

"You had a good time." He rolled them over onto their sides and held her close.

"Yes," she said, snuggling closer to his warmth. "I had a good time...a great time...a *fabulous* time." She kissed the underside of his chin. "When can we do it again?"

"Soon as my batteries recharge."

She grinned up at him. "And how long does that take?"

He drew his hand along the curve of her hip. "Today it won't take very long."

She leaned up on one elbow. "Is that a compliment?"

"No," he said, bringing his mouth close to her ear. "This is."

She felt his words from the top of her head to the soles of her feet. "Thank you."

"You weren't that polite a few minutes ago."

"I was greedy," she said, running her hand down

his chest, over his taut belly, then lower still. "I'm still greedy."

"Greed is good," he said. "I like greed."

She stroked him slowly, coaxing him back to amazing dimensions.

"Quite a trick," she said, feeling him throb against her hand.

"Glad you like it."

"I do like it." *More than I'd ever imagined.*

"Let's see how you like it from another perspective."

Holding her by the waist, he rolled onto his back. She laughed with surprise and delight as she found herself straddling his body.

"What's this?" she asked, her fingers touching a small bump beneath one of his ribs.

"Scar tissue," he said.

"Scar tissue there?"

"Do you want to talk or do you want to—?"

She moved against him. "Oh, I want to."

"You call the shots this time, Alexa Grace." His voice was husky, filled with promise. "How fast, how slow, how deep..."

She was dizzy with longing. His words came to her from a distant place. They had no meaning. The only thing that was real, the only thing that mattered, was the ancient, rhythmic call of the blood.

Connecticut

"SOMETHING'S WRONG," Ryder O'Neal paced the length of the communications center. "Brown always transmits a progress report at 0100, his time.'' He looked at the huge clock overhead. ''He's three hours late.''

The communications technician shrugged. ''So maybe he's hot on the trail of something and lost track of time.''

''You don't lose track of time in this business, Winslow. Not when it comes to communications.''

''Stuff happens,'' Winslow said. Despite her casual words, her dark eyes mirrored Ryder's own concern. ''You should know that.''

''Go to stage one tracking,'' Ryder said after another half hour passed without word from Kiel. The PAX operative assigned to the general area was somewhere out in the Bering Sea. He'd have to risk compromising Kiel's cover story in order to establish the current state of affairs.

''Affirmative,'' said Winslow, punching in a long string of codes. ''Stage one tracking, op 52AQ731, established as of now.''

LEXI LEAPED from the bed at the first shriek of the alarm. ''Good God in heaven!'' She reached for the robe draped across the foot of the bed. ''There must be a fire. I'll grab Kelsey, you—''

He was next to her in a flash. ''Calm down,'' he said, trying to look calm himself. ''It's not a fire.''

She broke away from his grasp and flung open the door. ''Listen to that! If that's not a fire alarm, I'll—''

''Don't worry.'' He grabbed for a pair of jeans and yanked them on. ''It's—it's the security alarm to my lab.''

"Your lab?" She stared at him in disbelief. "Someone's out there trying to break into your lab and you look this calm? Whoever it is might be heading toward the house this instant. I'm going to call the police."

"No."

"No? What do you mean, no? It could be some lunatic with an ax, Kiel. We have to call somebody."

He stopped. She watched as he took a deep breath and dragged a slow hand through his thick head of hair. "You don't understand."

"Darned right I don't understand. Sirens are going off, you tell me someone's trying to break into your lab, and when I say I'm going to call the police, you look at me like I just grew a second head. You *bet* I don't understand."

He pulled on a shirt, making sure he blocked her exit from the bedroom with the sheer size of his body. "It's my fault. I should've explained it better."

She listened as he told her about the sophisticated tracking system that linked him to a central clearinghouse in the lower 48.

"You mean you have to check in every day at one in the morning?"

He nodded.

"And if you don't, those—those sirens from hell go off?"

He nodded again. "Sounds crazy, doesn't it?"

It was her turn to nod. "What it sounds is unbelievable." She narrowed her eyes and stared at him. "If there's something wrong, I wish you'd tell me. I won't fall apart just because we're being stalked by a crazed woodsman or that Harry Blackburn who tried to jimmy the lock during our wedding party.''

He laughed and pulled her into his arms. She was unyielding. She didn't want to be unyielding but she couldn't help it. There was something very strange going on and she needed to know exactly what it was.

''No crazed woodsmen, I promise you, and no Harry Blackburn, either. I should've either reported in or disabled the system for the night.'' He stroked her hair.

She wanted to feel safe and secure. ''I suppose you did have other things on your mind last night.''

''You could say that.''

She kissed his chest. ''I did say that.''

The alarm blared again.

''Daaaaddddyyy!'' Kelsey's wail sounded from the other bedroom.

''I'd better go take care of things before we wake up the entire state,'' Kiel said.

She nodded. ''I'll check on Kelsey.''

BY THE TIME Kiel reached the front door to the lab, he'd called himself every four-letter word in the book and a few more for good measure. Of all the lame-brained, stupid, irresponsible things to do, this took the cake.

PAX was in an uproar. He'd let his work slide. And now Lexi had to be as suspicious as hell.

There was one consolation: it couldn't get much worse.

''The hell it can't!'' roared Ryder O'Neal when he answered the secured phone. ''We were a half step away from sending an operative out there and you know damn well we can't afford to pull anyone off their code-three assignments.''

''It was a mistake,'' Kiel said. ''It won't happen again.''

''It can't happen again, damn it,'' said O'Neal. ''What the hell do you think we're doing here, Brown, playing games?'' He named two of the latest in a series of Middle Eastern dictators to make inquiries into the possibility of purchasing nuclear weapons from countries once held by the former Soviet Union. ''Sooner or later, someone's bound to score. You're the best hope we have of disabling the material without creating an even greater risk.''

''I appreciate that,'' Kiel said, gritting his teeth against his rising anger, ''but something came up.'' The irony of that statement wasn't lost on him, but he was too disgruntled to laugh.

''All we ask of you is to check in every night. If you're not dead, you do it.''

''It won't happen again.''

''So what happened?'' O'Neal asked. ''Where the hell were you at one a.m.?''

''None of your business,'' Kiel snapped.

''Everything you do is my business,'' O'Neal said. ''You take a shower, it's my business. You go into town for milk, it's my business.''

''Yeah, well, this isn't your business.''

He heard O'Neal's intake of breath. ''Geez,'' he said. ''Don't tell me you and Lexi are—''

''I'm not telling you anything,'' Kiel roared. ''I'll transmit a progress report in the next five minutes.''

He would have enjoyed breaking O'Neal's nose, but he settled for breaking the connection.

LEXI WAS DRESSED and nursing a cup of coffee in the kitchen when Kiel returned.

"Where's Kelsey?" he asked, glancing around the room.

"Brushing her teeth." She looked at him, noted the tension around his mouth and felt a flutter of apprehension. "Is everything all right?"

"It's what I figured it was," he said, forcing a smile. "I reset the alarm."

She rose from her chair. "I'll get you some coffee."

"None for me," he said. "I'd better get back to work."

"You can't work on an empty stomach."

"No time," he said. "Gotta play catch-up today."

"Let me fix you something to take with you." It was her turn to force a smile. "I'm not much of a cook but even I can make a sandwich."

He shook his head. "Thanks, but I'll pass."

She looked at him. He looked away. Her heart felt heavy inside her chest and she fought to regain her self-possession. "I may not have a great deal of sexual experience," she said, "but you don't have to worry that I'll expect something from you just because we slept together. We said there would be no complications and there won't be."

"Shut up," he said, moving toward her.

She held her ground. "We got carried away," she

continued, ignoring the murderous glint in his eyes. "I, for one, can guarantee it won't happen again."

He grabbed her by the upper arms. "I told you to shut up."

She swallowed hard and looked up at him. "The hell I will. I know everything isn't as it seems, Kiel, and I know—"

His kiss was hungry, fierce, filled with heat and anger. She hated him for that kiss and she hated him because it didn't last half long enough.

"It won't be much longer," he said when he broke the savage kiss. "Then we can sort everything out."

"You're not really an environmentalist, are you?" she asked, suddenly certain of that fact.

"What the hell makes you think that?"

"I—I don't know." But it would explain so much. His odd working patterns. His lack of interest in the natural world around him. The alarms that went bump in the night. "The only thing I don't understand is how Joanna and her husband figure into this."

"Don't ask questions now, Lexi," he said as he started across the snow-crusted yard toward his lab. "You might not like the answers."

THE LAST THING Lexi felt like doing was strapping Kelsey into the truck and driving to Imelda Mulroney's house for little Matthew's birthday party, but Kelsey was so excited at the prospect of being with other children that Lexi didn't have the heart to refuse.

Besides, it didn't look as if Kiel was going to poke his head out of his lab for the rest of the day. She'd taken a deep breath and called him on the intercom to let him know they were leaving and he'd barely grunted a response.

"Coward," she said as she slammed down the receiver. Running away at the first sign of intimacy. *I'll have you know I don't like this any better than you do,* she thought as she paced the living room while she waited for Kelsey to finish in the bathroom. The last thing she'd bargained on when she agreed to this whole ridiculous enterprise was getting involved with the man she married. *Especially not sexually involved.* Just thinking about the things he'd done last night...the things she'd encouraged him to do to her...made her feel light-headed and warm all over.

And frightened. She wrapped her arms around her chest and looked out the front window. The only other time she'd ever been frightened was when her father died and she realized that, thanks to the provisions in his will, she might lose the entire framework of her existence. He'd wanted to push Lexi toward building a future for herself with a man who loved her. What he'd done was send her running headlong into marriage with a perfect stranger, all so she could lay claim to her money.

She'd believed she couldn't live without her penthouse apartment, her live-in help, Bloomingdale's. The thought made her laugh out loud. She hadn't so much as given Bloomie's a second thought since she left New York. She'd learned a great deal about herself in the past four weeks. She'd learned that she wasn't incompetent or selfish or flighty. At least not all the time. Faced with a very lonely man and a little girl who'd lost her mother, she'd discovered she had a heart. And she'd discovered how to share it.

Oh, Daddy, she thought, *that might be a better inheritance than the one you had in mind.*

Connecticut

JOANNA PLACED the slip of paper on the desk in front of her husband. "Bad news," she said, her voice tight.

Ryder looked down, read the typed message, then balled the paper in his hand. "Damn," he said. "It's starting."

"It's starting," Joanna agreed. "What are we going to do?"

"We have no choice," he said. "We have to bring them in."

"Today?" asked Joanna.

"Yesterday," said Ryder. "I don't like this. Now that Harry Blackburn's dead, we don't have anyone close enough to keep an eye on things until we can move them."

"How about—"

Ryder shook his head. "Still out on the Bering Sea."

Joanna pushed the secured phone toward him. "You'd better get on it."

Ryder said the code words into the mouthpiece, waited while the voice ID system analyzed and matched his speech patterns to the module on file, then dialed. "We still have time," he said to Joanna while he waited for Kiel to pick up.

She nodded. "A good twelve hours, I would think."

"We won't need that long. Kiel's the organized type. Once I tell him what to do, he'll have Lexi and the kid in the Jeep and on their way to the pickup spot." He paused, listening to the sound of the phone ringing in Nowhere, Alaska. "He's not answering."

Her eyes widened with concern. "Maybe there's a glitch on the line. Try again." He did.

Still no answer.

No doubt about it. The trouble had begun.

"EVERYTHING'S GOING to be okay," Kiel said out loud as the guided the car over the rutted road that passed for a highway. Kids came down with strange flus and viruses every day of the week. Just because it had never happened to *his* kid was no reason to think something strange was going on.

"Meet me at the hospital," Lexi had said to him, her voice trembling with fear. "We're taking Kelsey there as soon as I hang up." Apparently Kelsey had been stricken with a vicious flu bug during the birthday party for Imelda Mulroney's grandson.

He'd been out the front door in a flash. The car, provided by PAX for just such an emergency, started on the first try.

Someone must be watching over him, he thought as he wheeled into the hospital's tiny parking lot. Less than ninety minutes had elapsed since Lexi's frantic telephone call. Nothing terrible could happen in ninety minutes.

He ran across the light dusting of snow that covered the walkway, then burst through the front doors and grabbed the first person he saw.

''Emergency room,'' he snapped. ''Where is it?''

''Down the hall,'' the man said. ''Through the double doors.''

He was halfway there before the guy finished his sentence.

Lexi was standing near the nurses' station. She saw him the moment he pushed open the door.

''Kelsey,'' he said, blood pounding in his ears.

She laid a hand on his arm. ''It's bad, Kiel,'' she said softly. ''Very bad.''

Chapter Twelve

"Kelsey's temperature's still spiking," said the doctor, a dark-haired woman in her early forties. "It was a hundred and five degrees a few minutes ago."

Kiel slammed his fist against the wall of the waiting room. "Can't you bring it down?"

"That's what we're trying to do," the doctor said in an even tone of voice. "Believe me, we are doing everything in our power to stabilize her."

"Stabilize? What the hell do you mean *stabilize?* This was a perfectly healthy kid just a few hours ago."

"I realize that, Mr. Brown, and we're running a full battery of tests to determine the exact nature of this fever."

It wasn't good enough. It wasn't nearly good enough, but Kiel realized he'd pushed as hard as he could.

"She's my only kid," he said, meeting the doctor's eyes.

The doctor nodded. "I understand. Believe me when I say we'll move heaven and earth to bring that fever down into range."

''She sounds like she's not sure she can do it,'' he said to Lexi after the doctor disappeared down the corridor.

''She can do it,'' Lexi said, taking his hand in hers. ''Of course she can do it.''

''Things happen,'' he said as Lexi drew him over to the sofa in the waiting room. ''Her mother wasn't supposed to leave her but she did.''

Lexi's expression was unreadable. ''I'm sorry about your wife,'' she said, ''but that won't happen to Kelsey.''

''You don't get it, do you? Helena left us six months before she died. She packed up her bags, left a note on the kitchen table and walked out the door.''

''My God,'' Lexi whispered. ''I had no idea.''

''Neither did I,'' said Kiel with a bitter laugh. ''Not one damn idea in hell that she was sleeping with another man until I found that note. I wanted to kill her with my bare hands....''

''But what about Kelsey? Surely Helena would have wanted her daughter with her once she was settled.''

''Think again,'' he said. ''She signed away all claim to her own flesh and blood.''

''You asked her to do that?''

''I asked her not to. She said she wanted to begin a new life unencumbered.'' Again that bitter laugh. ''*Unencumbered.* Great word, isn't it? Kind of says it all.'' He met Lexi's eyes. ''You've shown that kid more love in six weeks than Helena did in eighteen months.''

''How did she—''

"Boating accident. Her boyfriend lived. She didn't."

They sat together in silence for what seemed like hours. Each time a nurse or doctor walked past, Kiel leaped to his feet, eager for news on Kelsey's condition.

Lexi held his hand. She smoothed his hair off his forehead. She ached to hold him close and share his pain. *I love your daughter,* she thought, wishing she had the right to say the words. *I don't think I could love her more if I'd given birth to her.* Another, more frightening thought surfaced.

And what about your husband, Alexa Grace, are you starting to love him, too?

"WE KNOW what it isn't," said the doctor two hours later. She listed a terrifying array of diseases. "And that's all good. At least we're narrowing it down a little."

"Is it bacterial or viral?" Kiel asked.

"We're fairly sure it's viral," the doctor said, sounding less sure than Kiel would have liked. "We'll keep you posted."

"I want to see her."

"I don't think that's the best idea right now."

"She's only four years old. She's probably scared to death."

"Kelsey is a very brave little girl, Mr. Brown. She's doing quite well."

"Then let me see her."

There must have been something about his tone of voice that told the doctor that he'd tear apart the hospital brick by brick if she didn't let him see his daughter.

"Five minutes," said the doctor. "No more."

Lexi hung back. "I'll wait here," she told Kiel. "You go."

He hesitated, then nodded and vanished down the hall.

Lexi paced the length of the waiting room, her thoughts a tangled mess of conflicting hopes and dreams and prayers and all of them centered on the man and child in the room down the hall. *I want to see you, too, Kelse. I just don't have the right.* She wasn't the child's mother or even a legitimate stepmother. Her marriage to Kiel was based on expediency not emotion, and not even the magical night she'd spent in his arms could change the fact that what they had was first and foremost a business arrangement that would come to an end one day soon.

He could have asked her to go with him, but he didn't. That omission told her everything.

"Lexi."

She looked up, eyes stinging with unshed tears, and saw Kiel standing before her.

"Five minutes are up already?" she asked, her voice uncharacteristically husky.

"No." He held out his hand.

"I'm not family."

"You are to Kelse."

She took his hand and tried to ignore the glimmer of hope inside her heart. She was still holding on tightly to it when they entered the ICU. How tiny Kelsey looked in the big white bed. An IV dripped fluid into her left arm while a tube down her nose kept her air passages clear. Her little face was flushed with fever and her eyes had that heated glaze that came with it.

"...hot..." Kelsey managed to say. "...want water..."

Lexi glanced at the nurse standing near the foot of the bed. "I don't know what to do," she said, feeling both useless and helpless. "I've never been around a sick child before."

Puzzled, the nurse looked at Kiel. "The child's birth mother is dead," he said in a flat tone of voice.

The nurse looked back at Lexi. "She can have some ice chips, Mrs. Brown."

One by one, Lexi placed the shavings of ice against Kelsey's parched lips as she kept up a steady stream of meaningless conversation that was more for her benefit than the child's. She talked about Mr. Rogers and Big Bird and sang all the lyrics to the Barney song while Kiel sat on the edge of the bed and held his daughter's hand in his.

Every now and then, Lexi and Kiel looked at each other and said with their hearts what they couldn't put into words. All of their emotions, all of their hopes, all of their prayers were being poured into the little girl sleeping fitfully in the hospital bed. They were united in spirit the same way they had been united in body not that many hours ago, and it was that union of souls that gave them hope.

THE HOURS PASSED slowly. Test after test came back with negative results. That would have been a cause for joy if only Kelsey's fever would break, but by midnight that miracle hadn't happened.

They drank coffee. They talked little. What could they say that mattered? It was enough to hold hands and to know that each found strength in the other's nearness.

He marveled that the spoiled brat who'd showed up on his doorstep with an attitude and a whopper of an unpaid bill had turned out to be a woman with a heart as beautiful as her lovely face.

She found herself moved by the love he had for his little daughter and wondered if he ever regretted that their marriage of convenience wasn't a marriage of the heart.

There was so much he wanted to say to her when the time was right. He'd thought this part of his life was over forever, that he was incapable of feeling the towering sense of joy that he'd found in her arms.

That forever was no longer one of his dreams.

And there was so much she wanted to say to him when Kelsey's fever finally broke. She'd come to him with nothing on her mind except her inheritance. Now she would toss it all aside gladly if it meant Kelsey would be her happy and healthy self once again.

If it meant she could stay with him forever.

"MR. BROWN." He heard the unfamiliar voice as if from a great distance. "Wake up, Mr. Brown. We have good news."

He struggled up from an uneasy sleep and glanced at his surroundings. Next to him, Lexi was pushing her hair off her face and stifling a yawn.

The hospital.

He sprang to his feet. The doctor was standing in front of him. ''Kelsey,'' he said, heart pounding violently inside his chest. ''How—''

''Normal,'' said the doctor.

He stared at her. ''What?''

''Normal.'' The doctor's professional demeanor slipped and she offered Kiel and Lexi a huge and triumphant smile. ''As in 98.6.''

''Her fever's broken?'' asked Lexi in amazement.

''Not only broken, Mrs. Brown, but vanished. Whatever it was Kelsey had, it left as quickly as it came.''

''You still don't know what it was?'' Kiel asked.

''Afraid not,'' said the doctor. ''I'd be lying if I said it didn't give us a nasty scare, but it's all over.''

Next to him, Lexi began to cry tears of joy and he found his own eyes welling with emotion.

''Now what?'' he asked, unable to suppress his smile. ''When can we take her home?''

''I know you're anxious,'' said the doctor, ''but we'd like to keep her another twenty-four hours just to be on the safe side.''

''She's going to be okay!'' Lexi threw herself into Kiel's arms as the doctor walked away. ''Oh, God, Kiel—''

He lifted her off the ground and swung her around. He felt as if he'd been handed the moon on a silver platter. ''Lexi.''

She looked at him. Her big blue eyes were warm, inviting. He'd never seen a more beautiful woman…or known a more caring one.

"I don't know what I would've done without you these past few hours," he said, his voice gruff with emotion. "You—"

"Shh." She kissed him gently on the mouth. "I lo—" She cleared her throat. "I care for her so much."

"I know." He held her close for a long, long time.

"I HATE TO LEAVE you here," Kiel said as he and Lexi said goodbye in front of the hospital an hour later.

"I'll be fine," she said. "Imelda promised to bring me a toothbrush and a clean T-shirt. The important thing is that one of us is here with Kelsey."

"I'd stay," he said, "but I'm so close to cataloging—"

"Don't." The look she gave him was unsettling. "I don't know exactly what you're up to in that lab, but I do know you're not counting endangered species."

For the first time, he didn't deny it. "You're part of it," he said. "You know I can't tell you more."

"I know you *won't* tell me more," she said. *Part of it? Part of what?*

He pulled her close and kissed her. For some strange reason, the kiss tasted of danger.

"I'll be back later," he said.

Lexi nodded. "I'll be here."

She watched, arms wrapped across her chest, as he drove away, his red taillights swallowed up by the night. What on earth had she become part of when she'd said *I do?*

THE HOUSE had been ransacked.

Kiel stood in the middle of the living room and looked at the devastation. Sofa pillows had been sliced open. Carpeting had been ripped up. Books and magazines and videotapes were scattered all across the floor. Even the ashes in the hearth had been sifted and left in a heap near the rocking chair. Everything that could be opened, torn apart, or removed had been.

He reached for the telephone and wasn't surprised to find the line had been cut. Okay. That was to be expected. But PAX, in its wisdom, had supplied secured and permanent lines to his laboratory.

He was halfway across the backyard when the sensor went off. The tiny microchip beneath the skin that covered his third rib vibrated a message that he'd prayed would never come. A bead of sweat trickled down his back as he remembered Ryder's final warning. *"Contact us immediately if the sensor goes off."* Not by telephone or fax, but by the ultimate in written communication, a satellite-based laser system that even the government didn't know existed. *"Bad news?"* Kiel had asked. *"The worst,"* Ryder had confirmed. "Let's hope we never need to use it."

His blood ran cold as he reached the lab and found half of the security system had been breached. Whoever it was, they meant business. He breathed a sigh of relief that both his daughter and Lexi were safe and sound at the hospital and out of harm's way.

He leaned forward, resting his chin against the support while retinal identification was taken. The green light flashed, and O'Neal's scrawl appeared across his monitor.

Operative found murdered.

WHO? Kiel wrote across the computer notepad.

Harry Blackburn.

That bumbling fool who had jimmied the lock during the wedding party was one of theirs? Geez.

WHEN?

Last night.

SUSPECTS?

Everyone but you.

NOT ALEXA.

We can't discount her.

BUT SHE'S ONE OF YOURS.

Nominally, yes.

WHAT THE HELL DO YOU MEAN, NOMINALLY?

We don't have time for this.

SO HELP ME GOD, IF YOU DON'T—

He was cut off by a sharp buzz emanating from the monitor. He tried to continue typing but nothing registered. O'Neal's words filled the screen.

Take Kelsey, go to the airfield and wait for the courier.

KELSEY'S IN THE HOSPITAL. ALEXA'S WITH HER.

Get Kelsey, O'Neal repeated. *We'll deal with Lexi.*

They closed the connection.

Kiel sat there, staring at the blank screen.

''Not Lexi,'' he said aloud as the old loneliness flooded his soul.

Not Lexi.

''IMELDA!'' Lexi put down her cup of coffee. ''Thank you so much for coming.''

Imelda's brown eyes crinkled with concern. "How is the little tyke?"

Lexi's smile was broad. "The fever broke last night. She'll be coming home this afternoon."

Imelda breathed a loud sigh of relief. "Saints be praised! What was it? Do they know? In all my days I never seen a little one get so sick all of a sudden."

"They still don't know exactly what it was," Lexi said, "but whatever it was, it's gone now."

"That's the important thing," said Imelda.

"Absolutely," said Lexi.

"You look worn-out," Imelda observed. "We're a hop, skip and jump from my place. Why don't I run you over so you can catch forty winks before you take the girl home?"

"Oh, I couldn't," said Lexi. "What if Kelsey wakes up? She'd be scared to death alone."

"Oh, I don't think that will be a problem," said Imelda with a smile.

"WHAT DO YOU MEAN they've left?" Kiel demanded of the day nurse at the hospital. "The car's in the parking lot. They couldn't have left."

"I'm afraid they did, Mr. Brown," said the nurse. "Mrs. Brown signed out your daughter, against doctor's advice I might add, two hours ago."

He'd never understood the word *terror* until that moment. Fear gripped him so tightly by the throat he had to remind himself to breathe. "There has to be some mistake."

She typed in Kelsey's name, then swung the computer monitor around to face him. "See? Your daughter was released in your wife's care. The signature card is on file."

"I want to see it."

"Mr. Brown—"

"Now!"

She made a phone call to the administrative office. "They'll fax me a copy in a minute."

He counted down the seconds. They were as good as their word. "That's Alexa's signature," he said flatly.

The nurse, eyes wide with concern, looked at him. "Are you certain?"

He nodded. "I'm certain." He'd seen that signature one month ago on their marriage certificate.

"I wouldn't worry, Mr. Brown," said the nurse, patting him on the forearm. "I'm sure they're home right now." She pushed the telephone toward him. "Why don't you call and put your mind to rest?"

"I can't," he said, dread sending icy fingers up and down his spine. "Our phone's down." A thought occurred to him. "If they'd headed for home, I would've passed them on the road." There was only one road from his cabin to the hospital.

The nurse's face brightened. "Oh, I know why. Their friend took them home."

"Friend? What friend?"

The nurse smiled. "Why, that lovely Mrs. Mulroney."

IMELDA MULRONEY'S HOUSE in town was empty. Except for the furniture, nothing else remained. No books, no clothes, no food in the refrigerator. Nothing.

Wherever she and her husband had gone to, they weren't coming back.

A red mist of rage clouded his vision. "Son of a bitch!" He picked up one of the maple kitchen chairs and pitched it through the window over the sink. Not even the sound of breaking glass satisfied him. He wanted to lay waste to the house but there wasn't time.

Think, damn it. Where in hell did the Mulroneys live before they came to Nowhere? Imelda had always been coy about the location of their "cabin in the woods." He'd chalked it up to a personality defect. Now he suspected it was a lot more than that. Her old man had been exchanging fish stories at the wedding reception. Kiel vaguely remembered hearing something about the best stream in Alaska running through their property. "Had to post the land to keep the hordes out," he'd boasted. "Before too long, they'll be bussin' 'em up from Seattle to take my fish."

He leaped back into the car and roared away from the Mulroneys' house.

Somebody in Nowhere had to know the location of that legendary fishing spot, and if he had to talk to every damn resident of the town in order to track it down, he would.

Connecticut

"WE FOUND HIM!" Joanna's cry broke the tense silence in the headquarters office.

"Where is he?" asked Ryder, his face drawn.

"His plane landed an hour ago. He's en route to Nowhere."

"Does he know the whole story?"

Joanna nodded. "He'll meet the others at the airfield."

"It's three hours since we heard from Kiel."

"I know," said Joanna. And longer than she cared to think about since they'd had any word at all on Lexi and the child.

"Did you look at the film of the break-in?"

Joanna nodded. "The guy was smart. He kept his back to the camera."

Ryder looked around the high-tech communications center and muttered an oath. "All of this equipment and we still don't know what in hell's going on up there. For all we know, we handed Kiel right into the hands of the enemy."

"Lexi isn't the enemy," Joanna said. "I'd stake my life on that."

"Don't, Jo," said her husband. "I'd hate to lose you on a bet like that."

"WISH I COULD help you, but I don't know nothin' 'bout the Mulroney place."

If Kiel heard it once, he heard it a hundred times in the next hour.

He went from house to house begging for information on Imelda and her husband and each time he came up dry. He uncovered their bank balance, how they liked their hamburgers cooked, and that Imelda wore support hose under her stretch pants, but he couldn't uncover one damn thing about the house they'd lived in before they moved down to Nowhere.

"Never thought too much about it," said Agnes Lopez. "They'd come down here every Sunday for church and be real sociable, but they tended to like their privacy." She frowned. "Though that sure changed once they moved here to stay. Imelda was a real friendly type, the kind who'd stop to help a stranger if he was in need. She was always droppin' in to set a spell and visit."

By noon he'd exhausted all of his possibilities. The only thing left to him was to fill up the tank of his car and start driving.

"Heard you been askin' about the old Mulroney place," said old man Packer as he pumped gas.

Kiel nodded. "Heard there's some great fishing up there."

Packer chuckled. "'Up there'? Ain't up anywhere. The Mulroney place is about thirty miles east of here."

Kiel thought his heart was going to explode as pure adrenaline shot through his veins. "You know where it is?"

"A man never forgets where he caught the big one, now does he?"

Two minutes later Kiel and old man Packer were racing east on Eagle Pass Road.

"Glad you brought your gun," Kiel said, noting the pistol in the older man's hand. "Just don't waste the ammo on me. Save it for the bad guys."

"You better be tellin' the truth, boy," said Packer,

"because if that little gal ain't in trouble, I'll make you pay for this!"

"Ten thousand dollars," said Kiel as the needle climbed past seventy. "Get us to that cabin in time and it's yours."

Chapter Thirteen

The cabin smelled of must and desperation.

"This isn't going to get you anywhere," Lexi said as one of Imelda's two cronies tied her to a straight-back chair. The ropes dug into her upper arms and chest, leaving her hands resting useless in her lap. Her mouth still smarted from the pull of adhesive tape when they removed the gag they'd used to silence her on the way there. "Kiel isn't rich. If you're holding us for ransom, you're going to be sorely disappointed."

Imelda motioned toward the rear of the cabin. "Put the kid in one of the bedrooms," she snapped to the bear of a man who carried Kelsey. God only knew what they'd done to the little girl; she'd been soundly asleep since they took her from the hospital. "And close the door so she can't hear us if she wakes up."

"I want her in here with me," Lexi said in an imperious tone of voice. The only weapon she had left was attitude. She doubted it would get her anywhere, but she had to try. *Kelsey...oh God...I'm here for you....*

"You want, you want," mimicked Imelda. "I

don't care what you want, little lady. There are things I want, too, and you're goin' to see that I get them."

"I tell you, you're making a mistake. Kiel doesn't have any money."

"Why does she keep talkin' about money?" asked one of the men who'd been waiting for them at the cabin.

"Because she's a good little actress," said Imelda. "It's almost like she don't know what kind of man she married."

"If you're trying to upset me, you're failing miserably," said Lexi. "Now bring Kelsey back in here this minute."

"Shut up!" Imelda backhanded her across the face, snapping Lexi's head back with the force of the blow. "No more games. He killed off one wife and I don't think he'd cry into his beer if he saw another one die before her time."

"You don't know what you're talking about."

"Oh, don't I? It wasn't an accident that finished off the first Mrs. Brown."

"She died in a boating accident. Kiel had nothing to do with it."

"She was murdered, right after she ran away from her handsome hubby."

"Liar."

Imelda smacked her again. "She ran off with another man, missy, and he made her pay for it. Sooner or later, they all make you pay."

A sudden, clear vision of Kiel's anger the night she'd pinned back Kelsey's hair with Helena's cloisonné comb danced before Lexi's eyes. The topic of

Helena had triggered his temper and that temper was considerable. There was a violence in him, a simmering anger that had been just below the surface from the moment they met. But murder?

No, she thought. *Please, no.*

She lifted her chin in defiance. "Even if everything you say is true, what does it have to do with me?"

"We didn't have to take you, lady," one of Imelda's henchmen said. "He ain't gonna give us nothin' for you, it's the little girl he's gonna pay big for."

This is a business arrangement, Alexa Grace... Marriage is many things, but convenient isn't one of them....

"Let the child go," she said, praying she sounded more certain than she felt. "Take her back to the hospital and I'll pay you whatever you want."

Imelda obviously found that statement hilarious. "You ain't worth a bucket of warm spit to us."

"Maybe not but my money is."

"We don't want money," Imelda said. "We want what he's got hidden away in that fancy lab of his. That's worth more money than they got in the mint."

"His lab?" Lexi's laugh was high, almost out-of-control. "He's an environmentalist! He counts migrating birds for a living."

"Right," said one of the men. "And I'm a rocket scientist."

...the triple locks on the lab door...the high-tech alarm systems...the sense of urgency that was part of everything Kiel did...

"Enough talk," Imelda roared. She turned to her

accomplices. "He's a smart boy. He'll be here soon. Let's get ready to welcome him."

They didn't bother to hide their paperwork or their conversation. All of which didn't bode well for Lexi's future.

I'm nothing to them, she thought as the minutes ticked by. *When this is over, they'll turn one of those guns on me and I won't be a problem any longer.* Not to Imelda Mulroney and her friends. Not to Kiel.

"...we've got to be careful," she heard Imelda say. "If somethin' goes wrong, he could blow us all to the next life."

They couldn't be talking about Kiel, not the man who'd held her in his arms and made love to her and made her feel as if the future was theirs for the asking. The man who loved that little girl of his more than life itself. Sure there was anger inside him. His first wife had walked out on him and their child. Who wouldn't be angry to see his dreams destroyed?

There's more to him than you know, that small voice inside her whispered. *You've known that from the very start.*

"Nothing will go wrong," someone was saying. "If we can't buy the secret from him, we'll steal it."

"We already tried to steal it," someone else said. "Either he gives it to us because we make him a better offer or—"

"Or we start hurtin' his kid," said Imelda. "That'll straighten out his thinkin' pretty quick."

KIEL LEFT the car two miles down the hill and made his way slowly, laboriously up the icy slope that led to the cabin.

"Stay here," he had told Frank Packer. "Watch for Kelsey."

"Wish you'd tell me more, boy," said Packer. "If I'm gonna get shot up, I want to know what I'm gettin' shot up for."

"I told you as much as I can tell you, Frank. The rest you've got to take on faith."

"Don't know why I am," said Packer, "but I guess I got me a soft spot for cute kids and beautiful girls in trouble."

"Me, too," said Kiel, shaking the man's gnarled hand.

"Good luck," said Packer.

Kiel nodded. "I'll need it."

They were going to kill him. He knew it in his gut. Whatever else happened, whatever they got or didn't get from him, before it was over he'd be dead. He understood that. He believed it.

If it scared him at all, that fear was buried somewhere deep inside his gut.

All he could think of, all that mattered, was finding his daughter. *And finding your wife?* How did Lexi figure in this? Had she set him up for a fall or was she innocent? When he saw her again, would he want to pull her into his arms and make love to her or put a gun to her head and make her pay for what she'd done?

The cabin was set deep in the woods. It wasn't much to look at but the same trees that helped shield the cabin from prying eyes provided cover as he made his approach.

They were expecting him. He had no doubt about that. The point of this whole thing was for him to find them. But he'd be damned if he was going to announce his arrival.

He dropped to his stomach and crawled the last few hundred yards, moving quietly between the trees, aware of the branches and jagged rocks tearing at his clothes and at his skin, yet not really feeling anything at all but the sharp edge of fear.

Was she in there plotting with them? Had she made it easy for them to grab Kelsey?

There'd been no trouble at the hospital. Lexi's signature was on all of the discharge forms.

She could be one of them. O'Neal hadn't ruled out the possibility. So many things about her hadn't made sense. Operatives prided themselves on their detachment. Lexi had thrown herself headlong into life as a married woman, even if she made it perfectly clear that the life she'd left behind had been a hell of a lot more opulent than his Alaskan existence.

He eased himself behind the tangle of bushes near a side window and lay flat, blood pounding in his ears, and he waited.

"HOW LONG are you going to let her cry?" Lexi asked. "She's been crying for over an hour."

"Let her," said Imelda. "So far it don't seem like her father cares too much if she cries."

"*I* care," said Lexi. "I want you to bring her out here right now."

''Listen to her,'' said Imelda, ''talking like she's the Queen of England, bossing people around.''

''Kid *has* been cryin' a lot,'' said one of Imelda's cronies. ''Maybe we should look at her.''

''She's been sick,'' Lexi said. ''She should still be in the hospital.''

Imelda laughed out loud. ''She's not sick. We slipped her something yesterday. Right in her piece of birthday cake.''

''Impossible,'' said Lexi. ''They ran every test imaginable and nothing showed up in the results.''

''And nothin' will,'' said Imelda. ''That's the beauty of it.''

A shiver ran up Lexi's spine. ''You couldn't possibly have done something like that.''

''Sure we could, missy. We have friends who can do just about anything. She'll be fine…this time. Don't go making the same mistake you made with your hubby—what you see ain't necessarily all there is.''

And that's when she saw it. The faintest movement at the window to her left. More a shadow of a movement than a movement itself but still…

Kelsey's crying got louder.

''Untie me,'' Lexi ordered, lifting her chin. ''I don't give a damn what you do to me, but I won't let you hurt that child.''

''Shut up!'' Imelda backhanded her. ''I'm gettin' tired of your mouth.'' She reached for a roll of tape.

Another flash of something at the window. Lexi's breath caught. *Kiel!* It was Kiel at the window.

''Lookie here,'' said Imelda. ''The little lady's

afraid of gettin' her mouth all taped up. Don't it break your heart?''

Her pals laughed. Lexi struggled violently, doing her best to keep their attention on her and away from the window.

''Don't do it!'' she pleaded with them. ''I'll stop talking, just don't tape my mouth.''

''Gotta do it,'' Imelda said, ripping off a long piece of adhesive tape. ''Since your husband doesn't seem to be showin' up, we'd better make some phone calls and see what's keepin' him.'' Her smile held more than a touch of malice.

The tape smelled medicinal. It felt even worse against the tender skin of her mouth. *Get Kelsey,* she prayed silently. *Don't let them hurt her. Grab Kelsey and run.*

''Kid stopped cryin','' Imelda said.

The youngest of her cohorts frowned. ''Maybe we *should* check her out.''

''No,'' said Imelda. ''She's quiet. If she starts wailin' we can't make our calls.''

''What if she runs away?''

Imelda's look was filled with scorn. ''Kid's tied up and the door's locked from the outside. Where the hell's she gonna go?''

''Far away from here.''

All heads turned in the direction of the deep male voice. Kiel stood in the doorway to the front room. He was covered in snow and brambles, his face was scratched and bleeding, his clothing was torn. Lexi had never seen a more beautiful sight in her life.

''The kid,'' Imelda cried. ''Get her!''

One of her henchmen made to push past Kiel. The guy hadn't counted on Kiel's powerful right cross.

"Anyone else care to try?" Kiel asked.

Nobody moved. Lexi was scarcely breathing.

"Kelsey's gone," he announced. "If you were planning on using her to break me down, you can forget it."

"We have your wife," Imelda said, sweat breaking out over her upper lip.

"Yeah, but I heard what you had to say about wives," Kiel said, entering the room. Lexi noticed the telltale bulge of a weapon tucked into the waistband of his jeans and her heartbeat accelerated. "Apparently I don't much give a damn about them, do I?"

"You tell me," said Imelda.

"Let her go," Kiel said, towering over the woman. "Then we'll talk."

"Like hell."

"Let her go," Kiel repeated. "She doesn't know anything."

He looked down at Lexi and for the first time he knew beyond doubt that she wasn't part of it. Whatever she was, however she had come into his life, she wasn't out to hurt him or his daughter.

He hadn't wanted it, hadn't gone looking for it, would have done anything to avoid it, but there it was. He was in love.

He'd always known he would give his life for Kelsey. From the first moment he'd heard her heart beating he'd known that. But it was different with Alexa Grace Marsden. The feeling had sneaked up on him, crawling into his heart and soul when he wasn't looking, turning a man who'd believed in nothing at all into a man who believed that anything was possible.

And he wasn't going to let this last chance for happiness end in a cabin in the middle of Nowhere.

Not without a fight.

He drew his gun and in the instant it took for his action to register, he pulled the trigger. The biggest of Imelda's two henchmen dropped like a fallen tree.

"Next one who moves gets it between the eyes." He meant it.

And now he wanted to prove it.

The second guy leaped for Kiel's throat while Imelda grabbed for the gun on the floor.

"Drop it!" he roared as she wrapped her hands around the weapon. "One more move—"

He fell back against the table. The guy knocked the wind out of him with a karate chop but Kiel managed to hang on to his gun. Not that it mattered. He couldn't get a clear shot with this bozo on top of him, landing punch after punch against his jaw.

"Take a look, hero. Look what I've got over here. If you don't hand over everything to do with your project, this is the last time you'll see the missus lookin' this pretty."

The guy fell off him at the sound of Imelda's voice. Kiel, gasping for air, turned toward her. Imelda held her gun to Lexi's head, the point of the barrel pressed deep into the soft flesh of her temple. Lexi's silky blond hair looked strange wrapped around the steel-gray metal.

"So this is it," he said, turning his own gun on Imelda. "Whoever blinks first."

"You already blinked," said Imelda. "What I have here means more to you than anyone in this room does to me."

"You wouldn't shoot her."

"Try me."

He could hang on to his principles and lose the woman he loved in a shoot-out.

Or he could guarantee her safety by turning over the best, most important work he would ever do.

He took aim.

Imelda jammed the barrel harder against Lexi's temple.

The veins in Lexi's forehead stood out in sharp relief against her pale skin. Her eyes never left his. It was up to him, all of it.

With one word he could secure her future.

With another he'd guarantee her death.

There was only one choice he could make. He took a deep breath, steadied his hand and—

Epilogue

Somewhere in Connecticut

From the air you wouldn't realize it was there. Tucked away in the mountains, camouflaged by dense woods, the building was all but invisible.

PAX headquarters had been the site of many sensitive meetings but never one more sensitive than the one about to take place in a few minutes.

"That's it, Mr. Packer. You are now officially debriefed." Ryder O'Neal rose and extended his hand to the older man. "We appreciate your help."

"Pleased to oblige," Frank Packer said, pumping O'Neal's outstretched hand. "I didn't do nothin' any good neighbor would do."

"You did a hell of a lot more than that," Ryder said. "You saved lives. We're in your debt."

Packer grinned. "Never knew all that duck-shooting would pay off like that."

When Kelsey had run down the icy hill crying that the bad lady was going to hurt her daddy, Frank Packer had locked the child in the truck, then hauled his seventy-year-old body back up that icy hill and saved the day. With one shot, the gas station owner had taken out Imelda Mulroney, enabling Kiel to finish off the second and last of her thugs.

"Have a safe trip home, Mr. Packer."

"That's pretty much a sure thing, Mr. O'Neal. Ain't many folks in Nowhere who've flown across the country in a private jet."

An aide escorted Mr. Packer out of the room. Joanna appeared in the doorway. "Is it time?"

Ryder nodded. "It's time."

"Don't ask me why, but I'm feeling nervous."

"Stay out of it, Jo," he warned. "What happens next isn't any of our business."

LEXI FELT as if she'd been waiting for this moment all her life. In truth, she'd been locked away in this strangely sterile building for less than twenty-four hours, but it seemed as if ten lifetimes had passed since that moment when all hell broke loose in that cabin. She could still feel the deadly pressure of the gun against her temple. She could see Kiel, gun drawn, staring death in the face.

And then the window had shattered as a bullet from Frank Packer's gun found its way straight to Imelda Mulroney's heart. *What were you going to do, Kiel?* she wondered. *What would your next move have been?* Would he have sacrificed his own future to save hers or would he have put responsibility before love?

She remembered screams... God, she would never forget those screams. Imelda's high-pitched wail...the low yell from her partner...her own scream that ripped at her throat as she saw her future vanishing in a haze of gun smoke. All of those dreams of happily-ever-after, of a real marriage, of watching Kelsey grow up to be a happy and accomplished young woman—all of it gone.

Everything from that moment on was a blur. A score of men had burst into the house, all of them shouting orders and collecting evidence. Somehow she and Kiel had been whisked from the house and taken to waiting airplanes. She remembered hearing Kelsey's voice calling to her, but she was unceremoniously pushed into the airplane before she could locate the child. Her old nemesis, Angus MacDougal, was at the controls but it was an Angus MacDougal she'd never seen before. He wore a uniform and a gold watch and a different air of authority than he'd shown before, and everyone on the plane called him "Sir."

"Surprised?" MacDougal had asked.

"Shocked," she had said. And that was putting it mildly.

What happened on that plane was even more amazing. She'd always wondered what a debriefing was. Now she knew. Every bit of information, every detail she could remember, had been talked about, listened to, memorized and recorded. It took all of five seconds to realize she was in the middle of something very big and very important.

And more than a little frightening.

When they landed at a private airfield in northeastern Connecticut, Joanna had been there to meet her. But there was no sign of Kiel or Kelsey.

"You have a lot of explaining to do, Mrs. O'Neal," she'd said as she embraced her friend.

"In good time," said Joanna. "I promise you."

Incredibly, Imelda was part of a far-flung group of radicals who made a fortune dealing with all things nuclear. While they weren't above selling weapons to interested parties, most of their millions were tied up in the illegal disposal of radioactive materials from nuclear reactors. Hazardous waste disposal was a billion-dollar business and growing, and that business would go the way of the Edsel if Kiel's theories on neutralizing radioactive materials proved sound.

Something Imelda's group was determined would never happen.

The most amazing thing, however, was the fact that all of this turmoil surrounded the man she'd married less than two months ago. Oh, he hadn't been counting birds in that lab of his. He'd been working on a way to make the world a better place and, if what she'd gleaned in the past twenty-four hours was true, he was darned close to succeeding.

"Well," said Joanna appearing at her side, "are you ready?"

Lexi laughed nervously. "What if I said no?"

Joanna put an arm around her shoulders. "I'd say it's time you got ready."

"Where is he, Joanna?" She hated herself for asking but she had to know. "Will I ever see him again?"

"Follow me," was all Joanna said.

THE MEETING ROOM was large and brightly lit. Kiel entered behind the aide who'd been dogging his footsteps for the past twenty-four hours.

"Take a chair," said Ryder.

"I've been sitting since we left Alaska," said Kiel. "I'll stand."

Ryder nodded. "How is Kelsey?"

Kiel smiled for the first time in days. "Great. No aftereffects from the poison, but that state-of-the-art playroom of yours will never be the same."

"Guess she's looking to go home, isn't she?"

"Yeah," said Kiel cautiously, "but that depends on where home is, doesn't it?"

"Should've realized you'd know what this meeting was all about."

"I don't have this IQ for nothing, pal." Yeah, he was a real genius when it came to reading the handwriting on the wall. Only this time, the handwriting was a road map and it pointed to parts unknown.

"Where is she?" It cost him a lot to ask the question. He'd never been good at wearing his heart on his sleeve.

"Turn around," said Ryder.

She stood in the doorway. She wore a pair of jeans, a cornflower-blue sweater that was at least two sizes too large for her and a look of uncertainty that he was damn sure matched his own.

"You look good," he said, too much in love to say anything else.

"You look tired." The concern in her voice made his heart turn over inside his chest. "Good," she amended with a small smile, "but tired."

They sat across from each other at the huge mahogany conference table. The damn thing was thirty feet long and ten feet wide, the kind of table that was designed to make a man feel as small and insignificant as possible. Good news for the designers: it worked. He hadn't felt that small and insignificant since his first year in grad school.

"We have a problem," said Ryder without preamble. "We can't let you return to Nowhere to finish your work."

"So I'll go home and finish my work," Kiel said. "The danger's over, right?"

"Wrong," said Ryder. "Until you've finished the last stages of your research, you're a marked man and it's our job to protect you."

Across the table, he saw Lexi lower her eyes. *Do you care, Alexa Grace? Do you feel the way I feel?*

"And the same goes for you, Lexi," Ryder continued. "You can name names, identify faces. You're no safer than Kiel is."

She looked up at Ryder. "Are you saying I have to go into hiding, too?"

Ryder nodded. "That's what I'm saying."

Kiel looked at Lexi. Lexi looked at Ryder. Ryder looked to his wife.

Joanna approached the table. "All of which leads us to the subject at hand—do we send you together or do we send you separately? It's up to you."

With that, Ryder and Joanna left the room, closing the door behind them.

Lexi said nothing, just looked down at her hands. Kiel's gaze followed. Her hands! There it was on her left ring finger, same as it had been since the morning they got married at Judge Moreland's office. She was wearing her wedding band. Was it too much to hope that she wanted to keep on wearing it?

It was Lexi who broke the silence. "Are you going to say anything or are you going to make me do it?"

He found it hard to breathe with his heart right up there in the middle of his throat. "Are you going to keep looking at your hands?"

She lifted her eyes. "No," she said. "I'm not."

"I love you, Alexa Grace." Her chin began to quiver. "You're hot-tempered, spoiled, too damn expensive for my tastes, and the one woman I want to spend the rest of my life with."

"I thought I'd lost you," she whispered as he kicked back his chair and went to her side. "I would have done anything, said anything, to keep you and Kelsey safe."

"Do you love me?"

She rose from her chair and stepped into his embrace. "More than life itself."

He held her an arm's length away. "Say it, Lexi. I want to hear you say it."

"I love you." Simple words whose meaning was anything but simple. All the joy, all the triumph, the very best life had to offer a man and a woman—it was all tied up in those three simple words.

"Do you love me enough to go into hiding with me?"

"Just try to get away without me." She fixed him with a stern look. "Does this mean we're going to have a real marriage?"

"You got it. A real marriage. The kind that lasts

forever. You've already cost me ten thousand four hundred and fifty dollars. Spread out over the next forty or fifty years, it's not such a bad deal.''

''Ten thousand?'' She swatted him on the arm. ''I know about the four hundred and fifty. Where did the rest come from?''

''It's a long story,'' said Kiel. ''Let's just say Frank Packer's bank account is looking better these days.''

Lexi took a deep breath. ''There's something I need to tell you.''

He grinned. ''You're pregnant.''

''Not yet. But I *am* rich.''

''Okay.'' He paused for a moment. ''How rich?''

''*Very* rich.''

''Like in millionaire?''

She nodded. ''Forty or fifty times over.''

''What the hell are you doing working for PAX?''

A funny smile tilted her mouth. ''Like you said, it's a long story.''

He listened as she told him. ''And what happens four months from now? Do you take your money and walk out on Kelse and me?''

''Never,'' she said, kissing him long and hard. ''And I can prove it. We'll divorce and remarry.''

He stared at her. ''That means you'll forfeit your inheritance.''

She nodded. ''I'd rather be poor and happy than—''

''How about rich and happy,'' he interjected. ''Let's not do anything hasty.''

She started to laugh. ''Are you a gold digger, Mr. Brown?''

"Just practical, Mrs. Brown. That money's yours. All I want is you by my side." He grinned. "And maybe that initial four hundred and fifty dollars I paid Angus MacDougal the day you arrived." He cupped her face in his hands and memorized the beautiful angles, the lovely planes, memorized the pink fullness of her lips and the blue of her eyes. *My wife,* he thought. *Wife of my heart.*

She lifted her chin.

He lowered his head.

Their lips were a whisper away when the doors flew open and a bundle of energy flung herself at their knees. "Daddy, Lexi! They gave me a puppy!"

"How adorable!" cooed Lexi. "A sweet little puppy."

Kiel took one massive paw in his hand and groaned. "A dog," he said. "A *big* dog." The dog that ate North America, if he didn't miss his guess.

"Every little girl deserves her own puppy," said Lexi.

"Please, Daddy!" Kelsey looked up at him. For a minute he almost swore he saw her bat her eyelashes. His funny little tomboy...

He looked at the puppy closely. "A male," he said. "I guess we have to keep him just to even up the odds around here."

He looked at the woman he loved, at the daughter he cherished...at the puppy chewing on his hand.

They could live in Alaska or Connecticut or on the moon. Rich or poor, successful or struggling. None of it mattered. All that mattered was that they were together.

For now. For always.

"What do you know," he said, drawing them into his embrace. "We're a family."

"One more question," Lexi said, tracing the curve of his mouth with the tip of her index finger. "What would you have done if Frank Packer hadn't shot Imelda when he did? What choice were you going to make?"

He didn't hesitate. The answer was as clear to him as the future that lay before them, theirs for the taking.

"There was no choice," he said, holding her close to his heart. "There was only you."

1. ALABAMA
After Hours—Gina Wilkins

2. ALASKA
The Bride Came C.O.D.—Barbara Bretton

3. ARIZONA
Stolen Memories—Kelsey Roberts

4. ARKANSAS
Hillbilly Heart—Stella Bagwell

5. CALIFORNIA
Stevie's Chase—Justine Davis

6. COLORADO
Walk Away, Joe—Pamela Toth

7. CONNECTICUT
Honeymoon for Hire—Cathy Gillen Thacker

8. DELAWARE
Death Spiral—Patricia Rosemoor

9. FLORIDA
Cry Uncle—Judith Arnold

10. GEORGIA
Safe Haven—Marilyn Pappano

11. HAWAII
Marriage Incorporated—Debbi Rawlins

12. IDAHO
Plain Jane's Man—Kristine Rolofson

13. ILLINOIS
Safety of His Arms—Vivian Leiber

14. INDIANA
A Fine Spring Rain—Celeste Hamilton

15. IOWA
Exclusively Yours—Leigh Michaels

16. KANSAS
The Doubletree—Victoria Pade

17. KENTUCKY
Run for the Roses—Peggy Moreland

18. LOUISIANA
Rambler's Rest—Bay Matthews

19. MAINE
Whispers in the Wood—Helen R. Myers

20. MARYLAND
Chance at a Lifetime—Anne Marie Winston

21. MASSACHUSETTS
Body Heat—Elise Title

22. MICHIGAN
Devil's Night—Jennifer Greene

23. MINNESOTA
Man from the North Country—Laurie Paige

24. MISSISSIPPI
Miss Charlotte Surrenders—Cathy Gillen Thacker

25. MISSOURI
One of the Good Guys—Carla Cassidy

26. MONTANA
Angel—Ruth Langan

27. NEBRASKA
Return to Raindance—Phyllis Halldorson

28. NEVADA
Baby by Chance—Elda Minger

29. NEW HAMPSHIRE
Sara's Father—Jennifer Mikels

30. NEW JERSEY
Tara's Child—Susan Kearney

31. NEW MEXICO
Black Mesa—Aimée Thurlo

32. NEW YORK
Winter Beach—Terese Ramin

33. NORTH CAROLINA
Pride and Promises—BJ James

34. NORTH DAKOTA
To Each His Own—Kathleen Eagle

35. OHIO
Courting Valerie—Linda Markowiak

36. OKLAHOMA
Nanny Angel—Karen Toller Whittenburg

37. OREGON
Firebrand—Paula Detmer Riggs

38. PENNSYLVANIA
McLain's Law—Kylie Brant

39. RHODE ISLAND
Does Anybody Know Who Allison Is?—Tracy Sinclair

40. SOUTH CAROLINA
Just Deserts—Dixie Browning

41. SOUTH DAKOTA
Brave Heart—Lindsay McKenna

42. TENNESSEE
Out of Danger—Beverly Barton

43. TEXAS
Major Attraction—Roz Denny Fox

44. UTAH
Feathers in the Wind—Pamela Browning

45. VERMONT
Twilight Magic—Saranne Dawson

46. VIRGINIA
No More Secrets—Linda Randall Wisdom

47. WASHINGTON
The Return of Caine O'Halloran—JoAnn Ross

48. WEST VIRGINIA
Cara's Beloved—Laurie Paige

49. WISCONSIN
Hoops—Patricia McLinn

50. WYOMING
Black Creek Ranch—Jackie Merritt

HARLEQUIN®

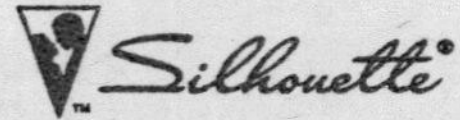

Please address questions and book requests to: Harlequin Reader Service U.S.: 3010 Walden Ave., P.O. Box 1325, Buffalo, NY 14269 CAN.: P.O. Box 609, Fort Erie, Ont. L2A 5X3 PAHGEN

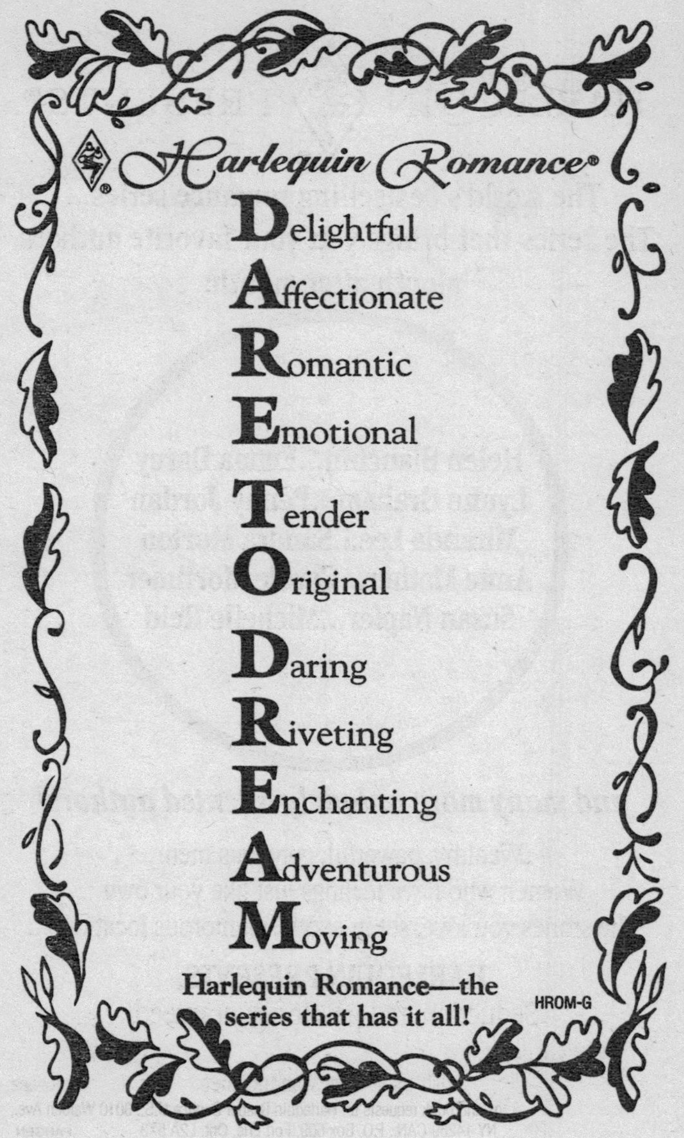
Harlequin Romance®
Delightful
Affectionate
Romantic
Emotional
Tender
Original
Daring
Riveting
Enchanting
Adventurous
Moving
Harlequin Romance—the series that has it all!
HROM-G